"So we grew together,
Like to a double cherry, seeming parted,
But yet a union in partition,
Two lovely berries moulded in one stem."

– William Shakespeare

Age is not a one-size-fits-all number. I'm seventeen, but there isn't a single seventeen-year-old out there to whom I can relate. Not even my twin sister, Ivy.

She enjoys being seventeen. She says it's not something you can change, so you might as well accept it. Even though I have a fake ID that says I'm older—which I made when I was fifteen so I could go see R-rated movies without a chaperone —there's no forging my real age.

I'm dying to be older, to be done with high school, to leave home for good, to get out of Kokomo. Ivy says she wants to live in New York, so I guess that's where we'll head when school's over. I don't really care where we end up, as long as it's far away from Mom, and as long as Ivy and I are together. We can't live apart, the two of us.

Just as I think about my twin, she bursts into the house, shaking spring rain off her umbrella. Ivy's not a fan of rain, but that's because it ruins her shoes and makes her hair frizz.

"I saw Dr. Frank today."

I lower my gaze to the bolognaise sauce. It makes a strange gurgling sound as it cooks, like a live animal drowning, but it's only ground beef. Ground beef isn't alive. Besides, there's more tomato than meat, because meat is too expensive. "Why did you see her?"

"I passed her in the street, Asty. On East Markland Ave. She stopped by Jo-Ann's to buy yarn for a scarf she's knitting."

I put down the wooden spoon. "What did she tell you?"

"She didn't tell me anything." Ivy shivers and dries her hands on a kitchen towel. "Do you like her?"

"She's nice."

Ivy's wet blonde locks glint under the cone-shaped ceiling lamp. "Do you feel like she's helping you?"

I shrug. "Sure." My twin is convinced I need help, so I keep weekly appointments with Dr. Frank, after which I swallow pills she prescribes. Not every day, but often enough to appease Ivy.

"She said you were more forthcoming than at the beginning of the year."

"I thought she didn't tell you anything..."

Ivy narrows her blue eyes that are a deeper shade than mine. "She didn't give me any specifics, Asty. Anyway, I'm so late. I hope Mom won't be mad. The salesclerk took forever cutting the samples."

"When has Mom ever been mad at you?"

Ivy winces. I smile to lessen her guilt. Mom likes Ivy; she doesn't like me. It's one of the only things that's not a secret in our family.

My twin retreats toward the veranda where Mom works around the clock, sewing quilts based on pictures customers send her. They're well made—I'll give her that much—but I don't understand how people can pay a couple hundred bucks for fabric copies of photographs. They should blow up their pictures and frame them. It would make more financial sense. I suppose most people don't have much financial sense.

Through the closed door, I hear my sister and mother speak, but I don't hear what they say. I put a lid on the tomato-meat sauce, turn the heat to low, and go take my shower while no one's occupying our only bathroom. I spend extra long under the hot spray, letting the water rinse away the scent of dried sweat from this morning's PE class. Some girls take showers in school; I don't. I always keep my gym clothes on underneath my school clothes, so I don't have to parade around in the nude.

Wrapped in my towel, I pad back into the kitchen to check on the sauce, which has thickened. Sometimes I feel like a witch, like cooking is magical. I throw together all these different ingredients and they bind in the most extraordinary fashion to create something new.

I put the pasta to boil, cross the small living room toward the adjoining veranda, and knuckle the closed door. "Dinner will be ready in five."

I don't know if they hear me because an audiobook is playing inside. They're always listening to books on tape. I wonder if it's to mask their conversations or if it's because they don't have much to tell each other.

I try the doorknob. I'm surprised when it gives. Mom usually locks her door. I peek inside. "Dinner will be ready—"

Mom shuts the bottom drawer of her sewing table with

her foot. The soft bang echoes against the glass walls of the veranda.

Ivy glances up at me, blue eyes wide. The waning evening light cuts a gilded path across the bright room, making Ivy's hair shimmer gold and Mom's gray hair shine silver.

"Dinner's almost ready," I say.

"I'm not hungry," Mom says. "Besides, I need to finish this for Friday." She gestures toward the fabric pooled at her feet.

Disappointment fills my stomach. I'm not hungry either, but I want us to sit at the table like a normal family. Even if it's merely pretend.

"Ivy?" I ask hopefully.

"I really should—"

My face crumples.

She folds what she's working on in half and then folds that half into more halves until it's just a tiny square of blue satin. Over the metallic drone of the sewing machine, she says, "I really should eat." She walks out and pulls the door shut behind us. "Want me to set the ta—" She stops in front of the small wooden table I've already set for three. I even clipped a couple branches from the buttonbush outside the veranda and put them in a water glass. The glossy green leaves give the table a splash of chicness. Ivy loves chic things.

"This is...lovely," she tells me.

Her words penetrate and linger in the tomato-and-garlic-scented air long after she's spoken them.

Steam blasts my face as I drain the pasta. "What does Mom keep in that drawer?"

"What drawer?" Ivy grabs a carton of milk from the fridge and pours herself a glass. She sniffs it before drinking, then searches for the expiration date. "Wow. This is a week old."

"Does it smell bad?"

"No, but it's a week old," she repeats as though I didn't hear her the first time.

Mom doesn't want us throwing out food until it smells. It's one of the few things we agree on, one of the few things she and Ivy *don't* agree on. This shared value hasn't brought Mom and me closer though.

"They put so many preservatives in stuff today. It's probably still okay to drink," I reassure my twin.

"Not taking that risk." She pours the milk into the sink, nose still wrinkled.

As the ribbon of white vanishes down the drain, I hear the nickels and dimes it cost clatter down along with it. I remain silent. I don't want to sound like Mom, always nagging Ivy about being wasteful.

I set two steaming bowls on our placemats. "So, what's in Mom's bottom drawer?"

Ivy drags her hand through her straightened curls. I rubbed some serum on mine like my sister taught me, but it did nothing to tame the frizz. I probably didn't put enough in, but I don't like putting unnatural stuff on my body. Taking medication for my mood swings is poisonous enough. I only take it every other day, but Ivy doesn't know that. She'd be really angry if she knew.

"Rolls of fabric," she answers.

"Then why does she lock it?"

She wraps a gigantic mouthful of pasta around the tines of her fork and shovels it inside her mouth. "This is really *really* good," she says after swallowing.

Pride inflates my chest and satiates my hollow belly

better than food ever could. But then I think of Mom's eternally locked drawer and suspicion supplants pride.

"Is it really only fabric?"

"Yes." Her voice sounds like an eye roll. "Aren't you going to eat?"

Pensive, I pick up my fork and dig into the gloppy red mess that feels like my life. This mess, though, I can make disappear. The turmoil inside me, that won't go away until Mom does.

Or until I do.

TWO

JOSH

"The sun feels so damn good. Classes should take place on the quad." I nudge Ivy, who's sitting cross-legged next to me.

"That's an idea," she mumbles, not paying attention.

"Vitamin D's good for the brain." I glance at my friend, who's bent over her phone. "It also makes facial hair grow. Did you know that?"

"Uh-huh. Yeah. Totally."

"Stop checking your Instagram feed and listen to me, Redd."

Ivy puts her phone away. "I wasn't checking my Instagram feed. I was reading about the new reality TV competition that's starting this summer. *The Masterpiecers*."

"What are people competing for?"

"Getting a free ride to the art school."

"Is that the place you want to go to?"

7

"Yeah. But unless I get a scholarship, there's no way I can afford it." She rolls onto her back. "I can't believe you're already done with your second year of college. That's insane."

I smile, feeling a quick rush of satisfaction. "One more year to go." I'm taking a bunch of summer credits to finish in three years, so I can apply to become a cop.

"Officer Cooper." Ivy makes a face. "Still sounds weird."

"Why?"

"*Because.* You'll be a law enforcer. You'll have a badge, and a gun, and stuff."

"Which will come in handy to get you out of trouble."

She snorts. "Like I ever get into trouble."

"Um. Have you forgotten the time you stole a pack of watermelon bubblegum from under the cash register of the CVS, and the salesclerk caught you?"

"Because Mom wouldn't buy it for me."

"And then Aster took the blame."

She rumples her forehead. "That was horrible of me."

Silence stretches between us as we both recollect the shopping expedition that started as an excursion to the movies—her mother wasn't actually taking us to see a movie; she was dropping us off for the afternoon because she had *stuff* to do—and ended with a slap that sent Aster skidding sideways and collapsing onto the sidewalk. I didn't have a cell phone back then since I was only nine, but I told their mom to leave before I had a passerby call the cops.

Mom was away at a baking conference in New York. She'd been planning that trip for so long that I hadn't called her, but I'd phoned my dad from a concerned bystander's cell. He came to pick us up and took us home.

Mom returned that night too—Dad had called her even though I'd told him not to—and she'd stormed off to pay Mrs.

Redd a visit. To this day, I'm not sure what happened, but Ivy and Aster ended up staying with us for ten days.

"Shouldn't have brought that up," I mutter.

Ivy bites her lower lip.

"At least we got a prolonged sleepover out of it."

The bell rings in the squat rectangular building behind us, signaling Ivy's lunch period is over. "Man, that felt quick."

"Time flies when you're with me."

She stands up and dusts the back of her jean cutoffs. "Why are you here anyway? Don't you have sun on your campus?"

"I'm taking Aster to the DMV to get her driver's license in an hour. Wanna come?"

"In New York, no one drives."

"This is Kokomo, not New York."

"But one day, I'll be in New York. You just wait and see."

Ivy is stubborn, ambitious, and overflowing with talent, so I don't doubt that one day she'll get what she wants. *Everything* she wants. I don't think she'd ever settle for anything less. We're kindred spirits in that way.

She readjusts the red bandana she's sporting to keep her hair back. "Bye, Joshy."

I roll my eyes. "Gotta stop calling me that. I'm not twelve anymore."

"You'll always be twelve to me."

"Go away. You're gonna get detention." I lie back down. "Plus, you're blocking my sun." We grin at each other.

She leaves, and I plug my earphones into my phone to listen to music while I wait for the other twin.

I MUST'VE FALLEN ASLEEP, because when I look up, Aster's crouched beside me, her incredibly light eyes roaming over my face.

"How long have you been laying out here?" she asks, prodding the skin on my jaw with her fingers. "You're lobster-red."

I heave myself up. "It'll turn into a tan."

"Burning is really bad for you, Josh."

"Thanks for the heads-up, *Mom*."

"I'm serious. I don't want you to get cancer."

"I don't want to get cancer either." I smile at her and take out the now-silent earphones. "Ready?"

"I think so."

As we walk over to my car, which I parked in the school lot, I notice her narrow shoulders are pulled tight, and her lips are squeezed into a line straighter than the markings of my parking spot. "What's up?"

"Remember that Pac-Man game I programmed for Ivy at the beginning of the year?"

Back at the beginning of the school year, Aster impersonated Ivy during an IT test. She's really good with computers, unlike Ivy. If she'd kept the code simple instead of adding cool features, the girls would probably have gotten away with it. Long story short, they got caught.

"The principal doesn't want to remove the low marks from our GPAs."

"That sucks."

She clicks her seatbelt on. "It especially sucks for Ivy. Her GPA's not that good. She spends too much time sewing with Mom instead of studying." She sucks in a breath and twists toward me, cheeks flushed. "Maybe I should record our classes. She loves listening to stuff when she sews. Then at least she could keep up with the curriculum."

I squeeze Aster's hand once before gripping my steering wheel. "You're so considerate."

Her cheeks become beet-red at my compliment.

"Look at that...our skin tones match," I tease.

She doesn't laugh. Instead she faces her window.

I didn't mean to make her feel bad, but I don't apologize because it'll fluster her more. Instead, I pump the volume of the stereo up until Jay Z's killer rhythm rocks the car and drowns out the awkwardness.

After three songs, I turn the volume back down and ask, "So who you going to Junior Prom with?"

She looks over at me. "I'm not going."

"Why not?"

"Because."

"That's not a good answer."

She picks a piece of lint off her baggy jeans. I don't know if it's her new medication, but she's lost weight. My forearm is larger than both of her thighs put together. Maybe I'm exaggerating, but she's definitely too skinny. After she passes her test, I'll take her for a celebratory donut run at Mom's bakery. She'll like that.

"Why aren't you going?"

"Because I don't have a dress."

"I'm sure Mom has a dress you could borrow."

She shoots me a horrified look.

"Oh, come on, Mom has great taste."

"I can't wear one of her dresses. What if someone pours punch over it? Or—"

"Sounds to me like you're making excuses."

"I'm not. Besides, Ivy's going with Sean, and I don't have a date."

I brake in the middle of the street. Thankfully there's no traffic. I pull over to the curb.

Aster frowns. "Aren't we a little far to park?"

I get out of the car, jog around the front, and sweep open her door. And then I get down on one knee. "Aster Redd, will you take me to Junior Prom?"

Her expression goes from shocked to crazy shocked. Even her mouth gapes.

I add, "Please?"

"Josh, you don't have to—"

"Redd, I want to! Come on. I promise to make it fun." When she still hasn't said anything, I add, "And I really do miss high school dances. It's the only part of the high school experience I miss." I don't, but Aster will go if she thinks she's doing me a favor.

She smiles. "Okay." Her full lips part wider over her perfect white teeth. "Okay, I'll go with you." A woman pushing a stroller passes by us. "Better get up before someone thinks you're proposing," she whispers.

When Aster smiles, she really is the most beautiful girl ever. She morphs back into the pigtail-wearing girl I chased through my granddaddy's sunflower field, the girl who shrieked when her sister asked to go higher on the tire swing, the girl who pressed a palm against her mouth when she laughed.

I almost forget she's like my sister, and I also almost forget she was diagnosed with schizophrenia five years ago.

THREE

Moments like the afternoon I went to the DMV breed fragile dreams. Dreams of love and a blissful future bursting with exquisite reds, sunny yellows, and cobalt blues.

For the millionth time since Josh asked me to prom, I close my eyes and replay his proposal. I shouldn't read too much into it, but what if—

Ivy barrels into our shared bedroom.

I sit up in bed.

She's holding something behind her back.

When she doesn't say anything, I ask, "What's going on?"

"I heard you're going to the dance."

I imagine Josh told her. I wonder if he told her how he

asked me. The thought makes a blush crawl over my jaw. I toy with my hair, twisting it into a long, coarse rope. "Yeah."

"I'm so glad because I made you this"—she pulls out something from behind her back—"and I would've hated to see it to go to waste."

The loveliest dress hangs from her outstretched fingers. It's fluid, sky blue, and shiny, like Springhill Lake on cloudless days.

"You made that for me?"

She grins even wider and nods.

I peel myself off my bed and walk around the brown sandals I kicked off when I came into my bedroom.

"Try it on."

I hesitate to take it from her. I'm afraid to soil its beauty with my indelicate fingers.

"I've been dying to see it worn."

I turn around to pull off my T-shirt. Ivy doesn't mind stripping when I'm around, but I don't like being naked or in my underwear in front of anyone.

"Hands up," she says.

I raise my arms, and she drops the floor-length dress over my head. It trickles over my skin like warm water. I wiggle out of my cargo shorts once the dress settles.

Ivy opens the closet door so I can glimpse my reflection in the long mirror. My eyes heat up.

My sister's smile transforms into a frown. "Do you hate it?" she asks softly.

Hate it? I spin around toward her. "Are you kidding?" I whisper hoarsely. "It's the most beautiful dress I've ever worn."

She rolls her eyes, but a pleased blush pinks her cheeks. "Wait till I get really good."

"You're already really good. You're way better than

really good."

She doesn't say anything for a while. Simply observes the satiny sheen of the fabric and the way it drapes over my light brown skin and jutting bones. "You could be a model."

I let out a soft snort. "Please."

"I'm serious, Asty."

I watch my reflection again. The girl in the mirror seems unfamiliar and yet completely familiar. It's Ivy; not me. The girl in the liquid dress is confident and stylish, the sort who would capture a boy's attention.

Trapped butterflies flutter inside my belly. Whoever said hearts were in chests never truly felt nervous and excited.

I squeeze my sister tightly against me. And then I cry because it's the nicest thing she's done for me in a long time. Not that she's ever unkind, but this is the pinnacle of kindness.

"Wait. What will *you* wear?" I ask, pressing away.

"I made the same in red."

The butterflies perform backflips. *She doesn't mind looking like me.* For some reason *that* makes me even happier than the prospect of Josh seeing me in such a stunning dress.

"And if anyone asks, they're BCBG originals. I sewed labels into them."

I don't know what a *BCBG original* is, but it seems important to Ivy, so I commit it to memory. In case someone asks. Although I doubt it.

No one ever talks to me in school.

ALTHOUGH I NEVER WEAR MAKEUP, Ivy adds mascara to my lashes and bright pink lipstick to my mouth. She's even relaxed my hair so that it falls in supple curls over my bare shoulders. Hers is blow-dried completely straight and dips down her spine in a swath of gold.

Between the shininess of her dress and the glittery oil she's rubbed over her collarbone, she resembles a bronze statuette of a goddess. Plus, she has on these high-heeled silver pumps worthy of one of those shops I would never dare enter at the mall because there are too many zeros on the price tag.

"I found them at Goodwill and spray-painted them silver." She grimaces. "Can you tell? Do they look cheap?"

"Nothing looks cheap on you."

"Yeah, yeah." She swats my arm, shakes her head. "What shoes are you wearing?" She starts rifling through my half of the closet. It doesn't take her long to discover that I only own two pairs of shoes: my beat-up Converses and the pair of brown sandals that are a size too small.

"Should I wear my sandals?"

Ivy bites her lower lip. "You know what, let's be fashion-forward and wear Converses."

"But...but your shoes are so pretty."

"Yeah, but they're not comfortable." She slides her feet out. "Want to try them on?"

I shake my head. I could never wear heels. I'd trip and fall, and I don't need more people pointing and staring.

She sets them neatly on the closet floor and pulls out her Converses. They're identical to mine, except hers are black instead of cream—the shoes were a Christmas present from Josh's parents.

When we make our way into the living room to wait for our dates, Mom's on the couch watching TV, fingers moving instinctively over patches of fabric. Sewing is second nature to her, like computer keyboards are to me.

"We won't be home late." Ivy walks toward the kitchen

and grabs a carton of orange juice. She pours out two glasses and hands one to me. "What do you think of the dresses?" Holding her drink out so it doesn't spill, Ivy twirls.

Mom looks away from the TV screen, takes in my sister from head to toe. She doesn't speak for a little while, merely runs her light blue eyes up and down and across my sister as though checking for a foiled stitch or an uneven hemline. "It's beautiful on you, Ivy."

"Isn't the blue stunning on Aster?"

As though remembering there are two of us, Mom's gaze surfs over to me. Her milky forehead crinkles like parchment paper. "Would look better if she actually ate something."

She often talks to me in the third person. I think she believes it'll offend me less if the criticism is delivered indirectly. A tiny frown clouds my twin's face. I lay a hand on her forearm.

Gaze stuck to my salient collarbone, she adds, "But the color's nice on her." Her eyes crawl up to mine and linger. Sadness gusts though them and sparkles like the dust motes suspended in the sunset light slanting through the living room window. Sometimes, I feel like there are a million things Mom wants to tell me but doesn't dare, or simply can't. Like two magnets, we repel each other.

The doorbell rings.

"Sean taking both of you?" she asks.

"No. Josh's taking Aster."

"Josh asked you?" Her translucent eyebrows arch.

I nod as Ivy pulls the door open.

"Is his mother making him?" Mom asks.

Josh stands on our doormat in a fitted navy tux that seems barely able to contain his pecs.

My heart gallops as his eyes meet mine.

"Hi, Mrs. Redd," he says tightly. "Ives." He saves my

name for last. "Aster." It rolls off his tongue like a deep gasp, like a prolonged heartbeat.

"Can you even breathe?" Ivy asks him, patting his stomach.

He unbuttons his jacket. "Barely." He winks. "The rental shop was out of suits, so I borrowed my cousin Vinny's wedding suit."

Headlights ignite our street, and then a red Toyota parks next to Josh's Camry.

"Whoa!" Sean gasps when he spots Ivy.

Sean has greasy blond hair. Every time I see him, I want to wash his long bangs or chop them off. But who am I to give tonsorial advice to anyone? Most of the time, I can't be bothered to style my own hair.

"Lookin' hot, girls."

Girls.

I blink.

He means me too.

"Eyes off my date, Braxton," Josh says, wrapping an arm around my waist.

"Bye, Mom," Ivy yells right before shutting our front door.

Some mothers would be snapping pictures or doling out unwanted sexual advice, but not our mother. I think she's glad when we get out of her sight, out of her house. When I menstruated at eleven, she told me to avoid getting knocked up, but that was it. No birds-and-bees conversations. No dating guidance. Not that I would've wanted any from her—after all, she wasn't able to keep our dad around—but advice would've shown she cared.

Josh opens the door for me, and I get in. When we pull away from our street, he says, "And by the way, Mom is *not* making me take you."

FOUR

JOSH

I really don't like Mrs. Redd. She isn't fit to be a mother.

I've thought that since the first time I met the twins in the McDonald's jungle gym. While my parents ordered me a McFlurry—I still ate those back then—I dove into the ball pool. Instead of landing on squashy plastic, I landed on something sharp and trembling. I dug through the balls, sending them shooting against the net, until I unburied this tiny body with a shock of wild blonde curls and tears streaming down her cheeks.

That was the first time I laid eyes on Aster Redd.

I remember thinking her tears were my fault, that some-how, I hurt her when I landed on her. At eight, I weighed as much as a thirteen-year-old. Once she calmed down, she explained she was crying because she couldn't surface from the balls. Her eyes had been so red that her blue irises appeared radioactive.

A second later, her lookalike trundled down the slide, waded through the multi-colored balls in a panic, and heaved her sister into a sitting position. I blinked a bunch of times, then muttered how much they resembled each other, and identical huge grins slashed their faces.

We played together until my parents said it was time to go, and then, as I was putting on my shoes, I asked Aster and Ivy if they were leaving too. They said they were waiting for their mother to come back. Mom asked when that would be, and they shrugged their knobby shoulders.

Their mother had up and left them there all by themselves. "They're five-year-olds!" I remember Mom telling Dad, puffing her cheeks out, way more furious than when I'd used my sled to glide down our stairs a month before.

Dad bought the twins and me Happy Meals as we waited for their mother. By nightfall, my parents packed us all into the suburban, excusing themselves for not having booster seats. The twins stared at Mom as though she'd sprouted a jetpack. They didn't know what booster seats were.

After sticking us all in front of the TV—*Ninja Turtles* was on—Mom called the cops. They arrived soon after. Even though I found them intimidating at first, they showed us their badges and let us touch them, and the woman cop, Jackie, told us about a robber they'd just caught trying to shoplift a gumball machine.

That was the day I decided I would become a cop. For the badge, but also because capturing bad guys stealing gumball machines sounded like fun.

From that day on, Mom, along with a bunch of appointed social workers, visited the Redd household regularly.

The girls know they can run to my mother with their

problems. But they run to me instead. They know I would do anything for them. Same way I know they would do anything for me.

I glance over at Aster, who's toying with the blue silk of her dress. She looks like a siren tonight, like a movie star, like one of those flowers that bloom only after sundown. Guys will be checking her out. I clasp the steering wheel tighter.

Aster doesn't fare well with attention. Maybe I should suggest we go hang out at my place or something. "You sure you want to go in there?" I ask, as I park next to the gymnasium.

She spins her head toward me, eyes wide, panicked. "Y-you don't want to take—"

I gather her hand in mine. "I *want* to take you, but I don't want you to be uncomfortable."

"As long as you're with me, it'll be okay."

"We can go home whenever you want."

I let go of her hand, and we get out of the car. Dozens of students are hanging out outside. Red dots glow in the darkness. Cigarettes.

As we walk past them, the looks start.

I latch on to Aster's hand. She tips her head up toward me. I'm usually good at reading her, but her emotions are muffled tonight. Or maybe I'm paying too much attention to everyone else to focus on what she's feeling.

I get a few *hey*s and a couple of fist bumps. I've been gone two years, yet people remember me.

Gazes slide up and down Aster's body. I tuck her closer to me.

"Nice dress, Ivy," Luke says, sidling up to my date. Luke and Ivy dated millions of years ago. He's still into her, but the feeling isn't mutual.

"Aster," she corrects him softly.

"What?" he asks.

"I'm Aster. Not Ivy," she murmurs.

Luke does a double take. "Serious?"

"Yes, Luke, *serious*." It's Ivy who says this. I didn't even notice she'd caught up to us.

Sean wears a trace of lipstick on his jaw.

Ivy grins at Luke, who's still standing there dumbstruck, eyes volleying between the two sisters.

Ivy smiles at his bewilderment. Or maybe it's swapping spit with Sean that's made her smile. Aster, though, has become rigid as a log. She's never been a fan of attention, especially since it was almost always negative. I know a thing or two about being bullied, since I was the butt of jokes during my chubby days. It was a long time ago, but the sting and the nickname—Hamster—never went away.

"Say the word, and we go home," I whisper in Aster's ear.

She shivers, combs a lock of hair back. "It's okay. I'm okay. Let's go inside."

"We don't have to."

Determination tightens her features. "I want to."

The enormous room vibrates with the sound of drums, electric guitar, and the high-pitched voices of the three girls on the makeshift stage. The school hired a band, like they usually do, but unlike at previous events, these chicks rock. They play a song from One Republic, but they've tweaked the rhythm, and it's catchy.

Ivy and Sean make a beeline toward the dance floor, where they melt into the crowd.

"Is Ivy dating Sean?" I ask Aster over the sound of the music.

"I don't think so, or if they are, she hasn't told me."

"Or it started tonight," I say. "Ivy tells you everything."

"Does she?" Aster looks up at me.

"Yes. She does." The mashed bodies remind me of the last time I partied on that dance floor. I feel like such a different person now. Confident and chill. I have college to thank for that.

"Are you jealous?" Aster's voice sends my gaze soaring back to her.

"Jealous? Of Sean?"

She bites her bottom lip and nods.

"I'm not jealous. Ivy's like my sister." I almost add *like you are*. But I don't.

I'm not sure why.

I spot a group of guys standing by the bar, ogling Aster. I narrow my eyes at them, but they don't look away. Instead, they whisper among themselves.

"Want to dance?" I ask her.

"Sure."

I lead her onto the dance floor and twirl her, and then I let her go. Aster has awesome rhythm. I'm actually surprised by how good she is. "Have you been taking dance lessons?"

"What?" she asks.

Her hands are in the air and she's swaying to the new song. I dip my face closer to her ear and repeat my question.

She shakes her head.

"Well, you're really good," I say.

She spins her face, probably to tell me I'm being too nice. That's her usual line when I give her a compliment. Before she can get the words out, before I can tell her to stop putting herself down, our lips brush. Startled, she pulls away, and so do I.

For the next half hour, although we remain on the dance floor together, the gap between our bodies stays as wide as the tube slide in the MacDonald's jungle gym.

I bridge some of the distance to tell her my parents are thinking of putting a Jacuzzi in our backyard. "Wouldn't that be awesome?"

Her eyes are a little red, which makes her irises stand out.

"Aster, are you okay?"

Her lashes lower. She nods, but there's no weight to her nod. I grip her hand and lead her off the dance floor. Her fingers are lax in mine. When we're away from the crowd, I tilt her head up.

"What's wrong?"

She closes her eyes. "I want to go home."

"Okay. Let me tell Ives we're going. Wait for me here okay?"

She nods, then folds her arms in front of her. I don't want to leave her alone, but I need to find Ivy, and I'm pretty sure she's sandwiched in the crowd. I don't want Aster to get locked between bodies and feel as though she's floundering again, stuck.

I find Ivy slow-dancing with Sean to a song that definitely doesn't warrant a slow dance, faces squished together. I tap her shoulder.

"I'm going to take Aster home. She's tired."

She angles her face to the side. "Did someone say something to her?"

"No."

"You promise?"

"I promise."

"Okay. Tell her I'll be home soon anyway."

"Not too soon," Sean says.

She smiles even though her face is full of concern. "Thanks for taking her home, Josh."

I rake my hand through my hair. "Of course."

She gives me a hug. "I mean it."

Before I let her go, I add, "Be good."

"Don't worry."

"I always worry."

"Well don't. At least not about me." She winks and turns back toward Sean.

I walk back to where I left Aster, but she's no longer there. Panic stirs in my gut. I check the bathroom and ask a couple of girls waiting in line if they've seen her.

One of them asks, "Who's Aster?"

"The weird twin," another one says.

My fingers jam into a fist.

One of her friends must feel my anger, because she adds, "Chill out. She's not here."

I run back into the gym and scan the dark crowd for blonde hair and a blue dress. I see a lot of blonde and blue, but I don't see Aster. Crazy thoughts catapult through my mind. What if a dude forced her to dance with him? Or maybe someone made fun of her and she's hiding in a corner of the gym?

After one last sweep of the room, I push out the doors into the warm Kokomoan night. My eyes snap to my car. A slender figure is standing rigidly next to it.

I sprint over to her. "Why are you out here?"

"I...too many people were staring at me." She's wringing her hands together.

I want to catch her hands and squeeze them in mine and tell her that everyone was checking her out because she was the prettiest girl in the gym tonight, but I don't do or say any of these things. "I think I'm too old for high school dances."

"Sorry."

"Why are you sorry?"

"For making you go."

I step closer to her. "You didn't make me go; *I* made *you* go. If anyone should be sorry it's me." Her head is tipped toward me, and her wide blue eyes shimmer. "Are you crying?"

She blinks, and one of her hands comes up and presses against her eyes, smudging her black eye makeup. I bet Ivy put it on her, because Aster doesn't usually wear makeup. "No."

I know she's lying, and yet I don't ask her why or who made her cry, because deep down I'm aware of the answer.

Me.

I made her go to a dance she didn't feel comfortable attending.

I thought I was doing her a favor when I offered to take her, but favors should make people happy. Coming tonight *did not* make her happy.

FIVE

Aster

"There's something wrong with Mom," I tell Josh in a low voice when I stop by his mother's bakery.

It's been three weeks since he kissed me. He hasn't mentioned it; I haven't either. I think he's afraid to start something with me, afraid it might complicate our friendship if it doesn't work out. Deep down, I'm afraid too. I can't lose Josh. He's everything that's right in my life. Like Ivy. Although she's also a reminder of everything that's wrong with it. It's not her fault that she's perfect and smart and beautiful. Just like my imperfections aren't any fault of mine. They come down to genetics and love. We might be twins, but we didn't receive the same number of good genes or the same amount of tenderness. I made my peace with this inequality a long time ago.

"What do you mean there's something wrong with her?" Josh asks.

I look down at the plate of mini donuts he's placed in front of me. There are three. The glazed, golden buoys of dough remind me of Josh, Ivy, and me. "The world isn't fair," I say, thinking about my faulty genetic predisposition.

"Aster?" His voice is so sharp I look up into his tanned, chiseled face. He turned twenty not long ago and has a man's face now. "What do you mean there's something wrong with your mother?"

"I think she wants to kill me," I whisper this so as not to alarm his mother, who's serving some customers a few feet away.

He jerks up straighter. "What?"

I press my lips together. "Inside her sewing room, she has this drawer she keeps locked. Yesterday, I was clipping the buttonbush when I saw her open it, pull something hard and black from inside. It looked like a gun."

"A gun? Why would she have a gun? Is she afraid of someone?"

I bristle at his suggestion. "I would never harm her."

His long dark lashes repeatedly sweep up and down over his dazzling green eyes. "I didn't mean to protect herself from you. I meant to protect herself from someone else."

"You think someone's after her?"

"Have you asked her?"

"I was afraid to bring it up. Afraid she might move it if I mentioned seeing it. I'd rather she didn't know I'm aware of it."

"We have to ask Ivy."

I shake my head slowly. "No."

"Why not?"

"Ivy and Mom are close, Josh."

"Don't you trust your sister?"

"Of course I do. I trust that she's protecting me. I trust that she's controlling and monitoring the situation. You know Mom's not always *there*, right?"

His forehead ridges, either in surprise or in concern. Maybe it's both.

"She's schizophrenic," I whisper across the small round table. "But don't tell your mom. I don't want to worry her."

He glances at his mother. For a second, I think he'll tell her, but his mouth doesn't open, his lips don't shift. Everything in his face tightens. "I won't tell her."

"Thank you." My gaze dips to his lips, and my pulse swarms and hums inside my veins. I close my eyes to harness the desire to lay my lips on his. "I need to get some groceries. I'm making pizza tonight. You want to come over?"

"I can't tonight."

I probably scared him with my talk of guns and schizophrenia. What sane person would willingly enter a house with an unbalanced, weapon-toting woman? Even though Josh wants to be a cop, he's not one, yet. I start to push away from the table when he says, "You didn't eat anything, Aster."

I stare at the donuts. "Right. I forgot." I'm not hungry, but I pluck one off the plate and bite into it. I swallow without chewing, then gulp down the second half. In seconds, I make the remaining two donuts vanish as well. I don't want Maggie to think I'm ungrateful for the free food she's always giving me.

I kiss Josh's bristly cheek and fill myself with his warm, liquid citrus scent. He smells like grapefruit juice and sunflowers, like rainstorms on a summer day. I smile at him, and then I smile at Maggie and leave the small bakery, holding the door open for a little girl with uneven pigtails.

She darts in on a purple scooter, wispy hair ribboning behind her. Her mother ducks in behind her, thanking me for holding the door. She has kind eyes and a gentle smile. She must be a good mother.

Déjà vu gels inside my brain like the foam spray I used in our bathroom last month to suppress an ant infestation. But it can't be a déjà vu because I've never seen this little girl *or* her mother. It's a vision of my future. One day I'll have a little pigtailed girl. I feel it in my gut.

I gaze back at Josh.

His eyes are on me.

Did he experience the same déjà vu? I dare to wonder if he'll be her father.

His gaze skims the top of the little girl's head, which doesn't quite reach the marble countertop, then returns to mine. Something gleams in his eyes.

He feels it too.

I want to stay with him, but I have to take care of my sister and mother. Someone has to do the grocery shopping. Our cupboards and refrigerator don't magically replenish themselves. So I leave, the baby-pink awning of Little Cakes fluttering over my head like a swaddle cloth.

I stare up. At its pinkness. And then I stare beyond it, at the pieces of blue sky visible behind the gray and white buildings of Kokomo, and thank whoever's up there for giving me visions of better things to come.

The name Violet forms inside my mind like a delicate soap bubble.

I don't know anyone by that name, which leads me to guess that it's another sign, another vision.

Violet will be my daughter's name.

Violet.

Violet.

Violet.

It plays on a loop inside my mind like a lullaby. It beats against my eardrums like a heartbeat.

Her heartbeat.

Clinging to the fragile gift bestowed upon me, I fill a basket with dry pasta and a few fresh items. I don't go overboard in the produce aisles because vegetables and fruit are expensive, but I grab a few peaches for Ivy. They're her favorite. I pick up some bananas for Mom, making sure they're still streaked green. She hates when they've ripened and bruised, even though she'll still eat them.

After paying, I return to my new car. It's a third-hand Honda with rattling suspension and shedding paint, but it's mine, which makes it the most precious thing I own. When I'm behind the wheel, cruising down roads with air conditioning licking the tip of my nose, I feel like the luckiest girl alive, like my new purchase was the first step toward success and change, like I can escape Kokomo. But I can't. I could never leave Ivy and Josh.

Stopped at the traffic light, I swivel and imagine a car seat strapped behind me. I love babies, but never considered having one before. Now, I can't stop thinking about Violet. I can't stop wondering if she'll have a little mole over her upper lip like I do. Are moles genetic?

A car honks behind me. I twist back around and find the light has changed to green. I press on the gas pedal and shoot through the intersection. A few blocks from home, I spot a woman exiting a shop. What snags my attention is the strawberry-blonde-grayness of her hair and the wispy texture of it. This woman has the exact same hair as Mom. When she turns around, I realize it *is* Mom.

I pull up by the curb and am about to call out to her and offer her a ride home, when I get sidetracked by the name of the place: PSYCHIC READINGS BY DONNA. It's written in pink neon lights set against a beaded curtain. Outside, two squares of AstroTurf have been laid out and topped with flashy orange furniture: two chairs and a small table.

Mom's laid her bag down on the table and is rifling through it. She hasn't spotted me yet. If I leave now, she might not even see the car.

But I'm a good daughter.

Even if she's not a good mother.

I lean over the passenger seat to roll down the window. "Mom!" I call out.

Her face jerks up, and her eyes, like laser beams, settle on me.

"Do you want a ride home?"

She walks over to the car, bends, and peers through the window. "Were you following me, Aster?"

I'm taken aback. "No. I was on my way home."

She grunts. Her mental disease makes her distrustful.

I gesture to the grocery bag in the backseat. After scrutinizing it lengthily, she opens the door and gets in, placing her enormous purse on her lap. I wonder if the gun's inside. I try to glimpse the contents, but she pulls it tighter against her.

I zip my gaze back to the road and pull away from the curb. "Did Donna give you some good insights into your future?" I don't know if she'll answer me, but it beats the stale silence. I should be used to it after seventeen years.

"I didn't ask about my future."

"Oh." I glance at her.

"I inquired after Ivy's. She's going to have great success one day. Lots of money. It'll pour down over her. And she saw twin towers."

"You mean like Ivy and me?"

"I mean like *the* twin towers."

"Mom, they crashed down during 9/11."

"I'm not an idiot." Her blue eyes have soaked up the shadows of the car. "Of course they crashed down back in 2001, but they still represent New York to a lot of people. The fact that the psychic saw them means New York is in Ivy's future."

Mom's always dreamed of living in the Big Apple, and she almost did, but then she got pregnant with us. She reminds us that we ruined her dream at least once a year. Usually, it's on our birthday, which is four days before Christmas. Her sorrow colors the rest of holidays in various shades of dull gray.

"And me? Did the psychic say anything about me?" I dare ask.

Mom blinks, which blunts the sparkle. "I didn't ask about you."

I suck at my teeth. I don't want to care, but I do. Sadness coils through me, laces around my belly and squeezes it like butcher twine.

"I always felt Ivy was going to do well for herself, but having confirmation is reassuring."

I'm so tempted to say *She's a psychic, Mom. Psychics are not higher beings. They're money-grubbing, cunning people who possess an affinity for human psychology.* I don't say any of this though.

During the rest of the car ride, while Mom drones on about Ivy's magnificent future, I think of my unborn baby girl.

Of my little Violet.

The sweet girl whose smiles will erase all the badness from my world.

SIX

JOSH

I call Ivy the minute Aster leaves the bakery and ask her about the gun. Mom's standing next to me. She keeps one eye on her seated customers and the other on my drumming fingers.

"Gun?" Ivy exclaims. "Aster thinks Mom has a gun?"

"Yeah."

"Why would Mom have a gun?"

"I don't know, Ivy."

I hear her walk around the apartment. "Where did Aster say she saw it?"

"In the sewing room. In your mother's locked drawer."

"She only keeps fabric in there."

"Under lock and key?"

Mom's bright red lips are pursed in worry.

"Only reason someone would lock anything up is to keep it away from others," I say.

"I know it sounds weird, but"—I hear something scrape and swoosh on her end—"Mom's weird. Look, I don't have the key, but when she gets home, I'll ask her to open it so I can check."

"You think she'll open it?"

"If she has nothing to hide, yeah."

The door chimes, so Mom bustles back behind the marble countertop to serve her customer.

I shove my hand through my hair, tugging at the short roots. "Ives, is it me or is Aster acting a little strange?"

"Strange how?"

"Distracted. Apprehensive."

A long pause. "Yes. Ever since the dance. I thought something might have happened between the two of you, but I didn't want to pry."

"Nothing happened." I sigh. "Has she been taking her pills?"

"Let me check." Her footsteps echo through the receiver. "Seems like she has. But maybe she's been flushing them down the toilet." She exhales a whistling breath. "What am I supposed to do, Josh? Grind them up in her food and feed them to her?"

"You need to talk to her. Maybe she has been taking them, but they're losing their effect. If that's the case, you need to get her on new ones." She doesn't say anything for such a long time, I add, "Or I can get her new ones. You're not alone, Ives. I'm here too. Never forget that."

She breathes. Just breathes. "Sometimes, I really want to leave this place. Hit the road and go somewhere. Anywhere. Preferably New York, but really, I'd take *anywhere*." Her voice wobbles. "I want to run away from both of them." Her low, gravelly voice sends a shiver up my spine.

"How about you stay at my house for a few days? You and Aster both?"

"That'd be nice. Are you sure Maggie wouldn't mind?"

"Mom's fine with it. She's giving me a thumbs-up." She's actually plating a brightly frosted cupcake, but I know she'll be okay with my impromptu invite. The girls have stayed over often in the past twelve years. "Call me later okay? After you check the drawer..." I remind her in case talking about her sister's and mother's conditions has made her forget about the gun.

I spend the next few hours helping Mom clean the bakery. As we lock up, Ivy calls me back.

"There's no gun," she says in a hushed voice.

I hold my eyes closed for a second. "You're sure?"

"Yes. And Aster confessed to having stopped her meds."

I squeeze the bridge of my nose and sigh.

"Yeah," she says softly.

"You want me to come over?"

"I think it might be overwhelming. Let me talk to her."

"Okay." I finally open my eyes.

Mom's staring at me, keys still dangling from her hand. Worry tracks concern into her laugh lines. She always complains about having wrinkles, but then Dad reminds her that not everyone gets to have them, that it's a great privilege to age, and she becomes okay with them.

"Is Aster okay?" Mom asks me.

I lower my phone and murmur back, "She will be."

Ivy and I will make sure of that.

AS DAD FIRES up the barbecue, I sit on the porch swing next to Ivy. She has her legs tucked underneath her and is staring at the screen of her cell phone. An old guy is revealing the identity of the contestants on the televised art competition she was telling me about.

Aster's in the kitchen with my mother. They're frosting Mom's world-famous blackout cake.

"Did you secretly apply?" I nod toward her screen.

"You have to be eighteen. So next year."

I watch the pictures of the nominees appear on her screen, but it's really boring, so I get off the swing and join my apron-clad father at the grill. He's talking with Jackie, the responding officer on that long-ago night who told us about the gumball machine theft.

At the beginning, my parents' and Jackie's interaction revolved around the twins' well-being. Then Jackie started joining our post-church Sunday brunches and over-the-top Thanksgivings.

I dig a bottle of water out of the cooler and gulp half of it down. It's late, but still so freaking hot. I run the bottle over the nape of my neck to cool down, then discuss Dad's latest construction projects. He runs a concrete finishing company started by my grandfather. He'd like me to take over, which is one of the reasons I'm getting a business degree, but I'd still rather be a cop.

"We landed the Discoli landfill commission," he tells me.

The Discolis own the largest private trash-collecting company in Indiana. There are rumors that trash isn't their only line of business. But their other line of business isn't legit, and thus no one talks about it.

"You don't say," Jackie says, sipping her beer.

"Don't start, Jackie."

She lifts one palm and holds it out in front of her. "I didn't say anything."

"Are they looking to cover dead bodies with cement?" I ask.

Dad's eyes grow as wide as the Portobello mushroom caps laid on the grill. "Joshua Cooper!" he exclaims, gaze zipping from Jackie to me.

"What?"

"That's not nice."

The Discolis are mafia. Everyone knows it.

Jackie grins at me. "That's my boy."

"I can see you've been rubbing off on him," Dad grumbles.

"How are they paying you?" I ask him.

"What do you mean?"

"Cash? Wire transfer? Gold bars?"

"Ha ha. By check."

"Uh-huh." Jackie winks at me. "You'll show me those checks, right? And you'll let me know if you find any bodies below the cement?"

I chuckle.

Dad sets the long metal tongs down on a mound of raw sausages and marinated lamb chops. "The checks will be certified. I would never accept anything else." He stares between Jackie and me. "It's a big project, which means a big paycheck. One the company could use right now."

I frown. "Are we in the red?"

"We're okay, but there are a lot of salaries and the market's been slow. I couldn't turn down the deal."

No one says no to the Discolis anyway. Either the money's too good to refuse or your life is too valuable to give up. There is no dream death, but ending up face down in a landfill is pretty much the worst conceivable kind, and that usually happens when you turn that family down.

"I'm not judging," Jackie says. "I'm simply wary of that bunch. Comes with the job."

"Did you tell Mom?" I ask.

Dad's cheek dimples as though he were biting it. He probably is. Although he and Mom discuss everything, and I mean *everything*—full-disclosure-no-secrets-everything— Mom fears the Discolis, like most Kokomoans. When she found out I was enrolled in the same summer camp as their son five years back, she told me to stay the hell away from him. Mom never curses, so using the word *hell* really marked me. Not that I would've hung out with the dude. He's a conceited prick who buys alliances with wads of dirty cash.

Dad's eyes dart behind Jackie. "I'm going to tell her. Eventually. Don't—"

"I won't say anything, but tell her," Jackie says.

I nod my agreement.

He runs a hand through hair that's the same brown as mine, but longer. He used to wear it in a ponytail, but thankfully chopped it off when I hit thirteen. "Not tonight," he says.

Mom crosses the lawn toward us, clutching a cake stand topped with a monstrous chocolate creation. There must be close to ten thousand calories in that thing.

"And people wonder why I used to be fat," I say, as she puts it down on the table, filling the humid air with the heady aroma of cocoa and butter.

Mom swats the back of my head. "You were never fat."

I snort. "Right. I was *pudgy*." I was fat.

Arms braced around a bowl of salad, Aster walks over to us.

"I think just smelling that thing is adding pounds to my waistline," I joke.

"I'll eat your share," Aster says, grinning up at me. "I'm starving."

"Glad to see you got your appetite back," I tell her.

I'm not really talking about her desire to eat cake though; I'm talking about her desire to live, to indulge. Ivy managed to get her back on her meds forty-eight hours ago by promising to get rid of their mother's "gun."

Already, Aster's a different person. Happier, almost serene. Her eyes are as cloudless as the dusky sky above us, and her smile as shiny as the sun poking through our picket fence. I want to freeze this moment, store it for the days that aren't as clear and bright.

If only her pills were a cure instead of Band-Aids, but there is no cure for schizophrenia.

Today is Mom's birthday.

She hates celebrating it, yet every year, Ivy and I make it a point to do something special for her. This year, we're taking her out to a fancy restaurant. It's Ivy's idea. I wouldn't have dared set foot in La Finestra otherwise. I wear the blue dress Ivy made me for Junior Prom.

When Mom walks into the apartment, both Ivy and I spring off the couch and sing Happy Birthday.

She claps her hand over her heart—well, over her handbag that she carries against her torso. "You scared me!"

Ivy smiles. "Sorry, Mom."

"Are you going somewhere?" she asks, brows knitting on her freckled forehead.

"Yes. And so are you," Ivy tells her. "We're taking you to dinner."

"Oh." Mom's eyes are so wide, I can't tell if the idea is shocking or appealing.

"Whenever you're ready," I tell her, pushing a strand of unruly hair off my face and locking it behind my ear.

"Okay." She eyes us again. "Why is Aster dressed like she's about to attend a red-carpet event?"

I suddenly feel self-conscious about wearing a floor-length dress.

"It's a nice restaurant," Ivy says.

"*You're* not wearing a gown," Mom comments.

"I felt like a skirt tonight." Ivy darts a glance my way. "But I'm probably underdressed."

"I don't have anything fancy to wear."

"What about the Diane Von Furstenberg wrap dress we bought you last year?" Ivy suggests.

"I sold it."

My sister's disappointment leaches the pinkness from her cheeks. "Oh." She swallows hard. "You didn't like it?"

"It was nice, but I owed someone money."

She probably had to pay that Donna lady or another psychic. "You can wear my dress, Mom," I offer. "I'm sure I have something else—"

Mom grimaces. "You're a size minus zero, Aster. Besides, I like pants better." Still holding her bag close to her chest, she walks through the living room and disappears down the corridor.

When I hear her door close, I whisper, "Is it me, or was she holding on to her bag awfully tight?"

"She sold our present," Ivy mumbles.

I sigh, then wrap my arms around my sister and hug her gently.

"Promise you'll never sell the dress I made you." Her voice is hoarse.

"Are you kidding me? Never! It's the most beautiful thing I own!"

She hiccups.

I hold her tighter. "I solemnly swear to keep it forever and ever." When I sense her breathing has evened out, I release her. "I should probably go clean up the backseat of my car before we head out."

"I'll help."

In the time it takes Mom to get ready, Ivy and I have rid my backseat of two empty pastry boxes and vacuumed the dried crumbs stockpiled in the groove between the seat cushion and the backrest.

"You look really pretty, Mom," I say.

For once, she's put on makeup, tinting her diaphanous lashes black and her pale lips mauve.

A blush highlights her freckles, adding another layer of color to her features. "Thank you."

During the drive over, Mom and Ivy discuss a new idea for a quilt while I focus on getting us to the restaurant.

The radio purrs a Christina Aguilera song in the background. I want to turn up the volume but am afraid to disturb the ongoing conversation. In my head, I sing along, and the music fills me, making me feel as light as a dandelion floret.

It was the song playing in the gym when Josh and I kissed.

We still haven't discussed it. I'm waiting for him to mention it, but maybe I'll have to bring it up. I wonder if I should do it over the phone or in person. I weigh the pros and cons of both. When we reach our destination, I still haven't made up my mind.

Mom presses her lips together before entering the dimly lit Italian restaurant. I feel as nervous as she does. The only one who seems perfectly at ease in our fancy surroundings is Ivy. I swear, my sister was born in the wrong family, but by God am I happy she was born in mine. I don't know how I would've survived if it had only been Mom and me.

Dripping candles are the main source of light in the small eatery. The effect is sultry, even though it makes scoping out diners' plates near impossible. I can't tell mozzarella from chicken. I rely on my sense of smell, and inhale the air that's flecked with paprika, fresh herbs, fried dough, and melted cheese. My stomach growls.

We are shown to a small table against a wall covered in flowery wallpaper. It reminds me of the butterfly print on our bedroom walls. The familiarity slackens the tension in my shoulders. I slide into one of the chairs and take the tendered menu.

As Mom and Ivy decide what to order, I slip my hand inside the little knit bag and discreetly count the twenties I peeled out of my pillowcase. Ivy contributed one and Maggie another—her present to my mother. I count five. I was sure I'd brought six. Could one have fallen out?

Cold blood prickles my face as I search the floor next to my feet for a folded green bill. I find none. And then I remember...

I used it to fill my car's fuel tank.

The realization tumbles on me like the Olympic bar Josh lifts at his gym, crushing, embarrassing, worrying.

Most entrées are priced between fifteen and twenty dollars so I wait for Mom and Ivy to order. My choice will be based on what I can afford.

Our waitress comes over with a pitcher of iced water,

which she pours generously into our long-stemmed glasses. "Are you ready to order, ladies?"

Ivy nods. She selects the lentil soup—$9—followed by the spaghetti carbonara—$19—while Mom asks for the buffalo mozzarella—$13—and the truffle linguini. I gulp when I notice the twenty-seven-dollar price tag.

"I'll have the chocolate soufflé for dessert," Ivy says. $6.

"And I'll take the tiramisu." $7.

Twenty-nine dollars left.

"And I'll have a glass of Prosecco," Mom tells the waitress. I quickly scan the price of Prosecco by the glass. $7.50. "And one glass of the Pinot Grigio with my pasta." $5.

I factor tax and tip. That leaves me with five dollars.

I don't see anything for five dollars.

"How much is a green salad?" I ask.

"Five-fifty."

Her answer crushes me all over again. With trembling hands, I hand the waitress my menu, blink, lashes sweeping back hot tears. "I'm not really hungry," I mumble.

"Aster, you have to eat," Ivy says.

Ivy must not realize I used one of the twenties to buy gas. Because I don't want to make her feel guilty, I repeat the line of not being hungry, and add, "I'll just have some bread."

"Bread is extra."

I wince. "A lot extra?"

"Two-fifty."

"Great," I say.

"She's struggling with anorexia," Mom tells the waitress.

A lump forms in my throat. I seize my sweaty glass of water and drink heavily.

"Mom," Ivy whispers, but Mom tells me how unhealthy it is, that it's a real disease. She enumerates all the effects it will have on my body.

I'll lose my teeth and hair.

My brain will be damaged.

My muscles will deteriorate.

I'll become infertile.

The vision I had of my baby girl settles over me like a balm. I focus everything I feel, everything I am on my precious progeny.

IVY INSISTED on sharing her spaghetti carbonara with me. She must have remembered our stop at the gas station, must have done the math and realized my refusal to eat had nothing to do with anorexia.

It was the best pasta dish I have ever eaten. My taste buds are still swimming in the richness of the sauce, in the saltiness of the crisp bacon pieces, in the creaminess of the Parmesan. I spend most of the ride home recreating the recipe in my mind so I can make it tomorrow. By the time we pull into our driveway, I have the list of ingredients etched inside my brain.

Cream.

Peas.

Parmesan.

Bacon.

"Watch out!"

Mom's shriek startles me out of my grocery list. Startles me, period. Something thuds underneath the car's front left tire.

I brake.

I don't dare move. None of us move. For long seconds, the only sound inside the car is our heavy, shuddering breaths.

I hit something.

Something soft.

Small.

I hope it's not one of our neighbor's children. I pray to God—if there is one—that it's not a child. I will die if I killed an innocent human being.

After an excruciating eternity, I click my seatbelt off. It releases me in slow motion.

I close my eyes, take three deep breaths, then push my door open.

Slowly, I lower myself to the ground. The pavement digs into my palms and bare knees. Soft mewing makes bile rise in my throat.

I crane my neck, spot a tiny form writhing in the shadows.

Not a child.

The crumpled body shudders, the fur shivers.

I catch the glint of glow-in-the-dark eyes and silver fur. It's a cat.

"Shit," Ivy says, crouching down beside me.

Sweat trickles down the nape of my neck, soaks into the blue silk of my dress. Her curse word doesn't begin to describe the horror of the situation.

"That's Mr. Mancini's cat," she adds.

"Is it still alive?" Mom asks, coming around the car.

"Yeah," Ivy says, "but I don't think for long. Shit."

I'm going to be sick. Vomit rises up my throat. I jolt out of my crouch and rush to the buttonbush plant and hurl my delicious meal. I taste the cream; it's bitter now. I taste the bacon; lumpy. I taste the pasta; bland and slimy.

"We have to put it out of its misery," Ivy says.

Rubbing my mouth against my bare forearm, I walk back

toward the scene of the crime. "I'll go"—my throat clenches—"I'll go get Mr. Mancini."

"I got it," Mom says.

For the first time in my life, I look upon her with gratitude. She's going to help me. She's going to make this moment less terrible. She'll take care of my cruel error. Fix it.

"Thank you," I whisper, at the same time as Ivy says, "How?"

I gape at my bleak-faced twin, then gape at my mother. *Right. How?* Mom pulls something out of her bag.

Something dark and sharp.

Something that goes bang in the black night.

EIGHT

JOSH

I don't think I've ever run so fast.

"Stay with me," I tell Aster over the phone as I jump over a curb, legs and arms pumping like karate chops. I lent my car to a buddy, and my parents drove over to a friend's house in the next town over, so there was no vehicle in my driveway. I thought about calling a cab, but didn't want to wait, so I started running the two miles separating me from the twins.

"She shot it." Aster's voice is a horrified whisper.

A loud voice barks through the phone.

"Our upstairs' neighbor is threatening to call the cops," she whimpers.

"It's going to be all right," I reassure her.

From what I gather, Aster ran over their neighbor's cat, and then her mother put it out of its misery with the gun Ivy told me she didn't own. Aster was right. Her mother has a gun.

None of us took her seriously.

"Is Mr. Mancini still there?" I ask through labored breaths. I thought I was in good shape, but I can barely breathe.

"He's talking with Mom," she murmurs. There are tears in her voice. I can hear them. They coat her vocal cords in something hot and thick.

"I'm almost there. Where's Ivy?"

"She's talking to the neighbors."

"Okay. Hold on. I'm around the corner." I skip over a low hedge and hang a sharp left on Mulberry Street.

Moonlight outlines six dark figures.

Aster clutches her phone with one hand and hugs her waist with the other. Sobs make her dress tremble like a ribbon.

I lower my cell phone, then crush her against me. She soaks the collar of my already-damp T-shirt with tears. I rub her back, and then, when I feel she's calmed down, I pull away. Tucking her hand in mine, I guide her toward the others.

Mr. Mancini's hunched over a small, curled form lying in a black puddle.

"Hey," I tell Ivy softly. Then, I nod to the middle-aged couple who lives over the Redds' apartment. They stand in matching navy bathrobes and matching white slippers. The man's arms are folded tightly over his chest, while his wife just looks spooked with her wide eyes and half-open mouth. She's holding her phone in her hands. "Did you call the cops?" I ask them.

"Not yet, but this crazy woman has a gun."

Mrs. Redd spears him with a look. "Which I used to fix a

dire situation."

"Do you even have a license to carry?" the man asks.

"Of course I do." A nerve ticks in her freckled jaw.

"I don't feel safe knowing you have a gun," he says.

"Oh, come on, everyone on this fucking street has a gun," Mrs. Redd says.

"Where is it?" I ask.

Ivy points to her mother's right hand. It's a Glock. Those don't come with safeties—Jackie taught me about guns. And Mrs. Redd's index finger is still dangerously close to the trigger. So as not to alarm anyone, I ask if I can take it from her.

She jerks her hand up. I take an involuntary step back. Actually, it's totally voluntary. After all, she's aiming a gun straight at me. I raise my palms.

"Take it." She all but throws it at me.

Releasing Aster's hand, I rip it from Mrs. Redd's fingers and eject the magazine, then stuff both inside my pockets. Not that I think it will accidentally fire but why risk it?

"We should call the police, Steve," the wife tells her husband. "I'm going to call them." She starts typing numbers on her phone.

"Please...please don't," I say. "There's no more threat. I'll take the gun to the precinct—"

"Who says she don't have another one stashed away?" the man asks.

"I don't have another one." Mrs. Redd's voice is angry. A little wobbly.

"Please don't involve the police?" Ivy pleads. "Please. They'll take her away. Please."

Her series of pleases rattles their resolve. "Mr. Mancini, you want us to call the cops?"

Mr. Mancini lets out a wheezing sound. "No. It's all right. Thank you for your concern." His gaze brushes over them, then over me, then returns to the crumpled mass of fur at his feet. "Bullet," he whispers, his voice hoarse. I think he's telling me how the cat died, but then he says it again—"Oh, Bullet"—and I recall it's the feline's name.

The neighbors finally return upstairs, grumbling loudly.

Ivy releases a sigh of relief while I contemplate how I can help Mr. Mancini. I spy a cardboard box in the neighbors' trashcan. I wrestle it out and bring it over.

The old man straightens and lifts slick, perplexed eyes toward me, then toward the box. I put the box down and, trying my hardest not to flinch or gag, I slide my fingers under the cat's weightless, broken body.

Sticky, hot blood coats my hands, runs through my fingers, drips over the gray pavement. As delicately as possible, I place the cat in the cardboard box.

I breathe through my mouth to avoid smelling the blood that's everywhere. "Mrs. Redd, could I use your sink to wash my hands?"

She makes no move to open her front door. Aster leads me inside. As I step over the threshold, Ivy asks Mr. Mancini if he's going to press charges. I don't catch his answer.

Could he press charges? He could probably ask for money, but they don't have any, and he knows it. *Crap.* I rush to the kitchen sink and use a heap of soap. Way more than necessary. My hands still don't feel clean when I dry them against my sweatpants.

I grab an upturned glass from the cupboard over the sink and fill it with cold water that I gulp down. And then I pour a second glass for Aster and force her to sit on the couch and drink it.

"I'll be right back. Stay here." I jog back out.

Mancini's crossing the street toward his apartment. The box is no longer there, so I assume he took Bullet with him.

"What did he say?" I ask Ivy.

"He says it was an accident." Her blue eyes are wide, but neither red like her sister's, nor vacant like her mother's. "It *was* an accident."

The car was; the bullet wasn't. I don't bring this up. Besides, I doubt the cat could've survived the weight of Aster's car. Even if it really had nine lives.

Ivy rubs the arms of her bobbing mother. "Mom, it's okay."

"Get her inside, Ives," I say softly. "I'll go see Mr. Mancini."

"I need to clean up the blood."

"I'll do it after. Go."

She leads her mother inside.

As I walk across the street, the weapon bangs against my thigh.

Mancini's door is ajar. Still, I knock. On his dining room table rests the box. I can't see Bullet from my vantage point—not that I want to. "Mr. Mancini, can I help with something?"

He's half-in, half-out of a closet. Things crash and thud inside. He mumbles curse words. Finally, he turns around, a shovel in his knobby fingers. "Let me do that," I offer, walking over to him. "Where do you want the hole?"

"In the backyard," he croaks. "Under the lilac tree."

I extricate the shovel from his trembling hands, then stride out and around the house to his small backyard. There is only one tree back there, thin-trunked and loaded with white blossoms that suffuse the night air.

Lifting weights three times a week makes shoveling the soft earth swift. In ten minutes, the hole is deep enough for the box. I return to the house to get Mancini. He's sitting at his kitchen table, fingers intertwined, forehead lowered. Maybe he's praying.

I clear my throat so I don't startle him. "It's ready."

"Thank you." He presses away from the table, folds the flaps of the cardboard box, then reverentially gathers it in his arms and carries it out. I follow him with the shovel.

He sets the box down in the little hole, tears a cluster of white blossoms from a branch of the lilac tree, and lays it on top of Bullet's final resting place. "He was my daughter's cat. Never liked the thing at first. But then she left, and he stayed, and"—his voice snags—"and well, I grew attached to the mangy fur ball. He was loyal as hell. Mark my words, Josh, animals are better than people. They'll like you with all your goddamn flaws, and they won't leave..." The old man makes a noise that sounds like a choked howl.

I sniffle. I'm not sure if it's the tree or Mancini's emotional eulogy. Maybe it's both. I rub my eyes with the back of my hands, then ask if he's ready for me to pack the earth around the box.

"I'll do it, Joshua. Thank you. Now go see to the women. They need you more than I do."

The twins' old neighbor always struck me as a hardened widower who cared more about his NRA membership than about real people. Tonight, though, I see another facet of the man: kindness.

"Thanks for not pressing charges." I give him the shovel.

He nods and wraps arthritic fingers around the wooden handle. "Wasn't premeditated."

I let out a heavy breath and leave the man alone with his lost friend.

When I step back into the twins' house, it's quiet. Ivy's making tea in the kitchen while Aster and her mom sit on opposite ends of the L-shaped couch, gazes cast downward. None of them speak. Shell-shocked. Lost in thought.

"She *did* have a gun," I murmur to Ivy. The electric kettle gushes, drowning out my voice. I don't mean to sound accusing, but I realize that's exactly how I sound.

She twists a long lock of blonde hair over and over around her finger. "I know."

"Does she really have a license to carry?"

Ivy shakes her head no just as the kettle clicks off.

"Where'd she get it?" This comes out louder than intended.

"I found it in the pocket of one of my coats," Mrs. Redd answers, her voice ringing through the quiet apartment.

I spin around like a swizzle stick.

Aster once told me their mother had a passion for coats: fur, trench, leather, wool. She had several of each. Winters in Kokomo are glacial, but does a person need that many coats? Surely not. Especially when her daughters can barely afford one good one.

"I was cleaning my closet"—she's bobbing forward and back, forward and back—"when I felt a bulge in a pocket."

"Where did it come from?"

"Don't know." Her voice shakes in time with her swaying body. "Someone must have planted it there."

Ivy walks out of the kitchen gripping a mug of tea. She sets it in front of her mother on the coffee table, then grabs her hands and whispers words I can't hear.

"Why would someone put a gun in your closet?" I ask, coming to sit next to Aster, who seems frozen in place. She hasn't looked up once since I walked in.

"To frame me." She stares at Aster. "Someone must want to frame me." She's no longer bobbing. She's suddenly calm. "Maybe it's been used in a murder." She says this so flatly it makes my back snap straight and trails cold fingers of fear up my spine.

I lay a shaky hand on the gun concealed in my sweatpants. What if it *is* a murder weapon? It has my prints all over it now. I shove the thought away. Jackie would believe me when I tell her I never fired it. "Have you checked who it's registered to?"

"No. I didn't want to go asking too many questions," she says, still fixing Aster with a dead-eyed stare. Does Mrs. Redd know her daughter told me about the gun?

Aster's head jerks up. "Then why were you carrying it around?"

"Because I couldn't very well leave it here. Social services are already crawling up my ass. If they found a gun, they'd haul me off to the nuthouse."

Ivy gasps; Aster doesn't make a single sound.

"But perhaps that's what you want, Aster."

Aster's body stiffens until she is only a stack of bones, no more soft flesh.

"Mom!" Ivy drops her mother's hands and stares at her in horror.

"What? You don't think your sister's capable of that? Don't you see how she's always watching us? Always listening to us?"

A tear courses down Aster's gaunt cheek. And then another. And another. I wrap an arm around her shoulder and pull her in close.

I'm shaking now, but out of anger. If my mother heard this accusation, she'd wring Mrs. Redd's scrawny, pasty neck. "Your daughter would never do that to you."

She snorts. "You should be careful who you trust, Joshua."

I tighten my hold on Aster, then whisper in her ear, "Go pack a bag."

Aster squeezes her lips together, squeezes her lids closed, squeezes my hand. And then she gets up and walks to her bedroom.

I meet Ivy's gaze. She stands up and follows Aster. I hear them talk quietly.

"My daughter's not right in the head. And she has it out for me. I bet she planted that weapon in my closet."

"She still wouldn't do that," I repeat.

"She has money to pay for a fancy dinner. She probably has money to buy a gun. You have any clue where she's getting all that money?"

"Tips from waitressing jobs. Aster's a hard worker."

"Waitresses don't make that much money. Unless they're offering additional services."

Her insinuation raises my hackles. "Aster's never prostituted herself," I hiss.

"And you would know that how, Joshua? Are you *always* with her? Don't you have a life?"

Blood pumps furiously in my veins. I stand up, curl my fingers into fists, lock them at my sides.

"Are you going to hit me?" she asks.

"I would never hit a woman." Right now, I'm willing to make an exception.

"Are you screwing my daughter, Joshua?"

I'm too startled by her question to answer. Besides, it's none of her business.

"'Cause if you are, and you knock her up, you're in charge of her *and* the baby."

I hope the look I give her is as cutting as the pocketknife Dad keeps in the glovebox of his car.

"I'm ready," Aster says softly.

I hold out a hand, praying she didn't hear her mother's last comment.

Aster hoists her backpack over her shoulder. It looks heavier than she does. I pluck it off her arm and carry it. "You want to come too?" I ask Ivy who's standing in the little hallway.

She shoots me a longing look. "Mom needs me."

Trapping Aster's icy hand, I head out the door. I feel bad leaving my friend behind with this monster, but I know Ivy can control her mother. She's like a horse whisperer, but for schizophrenics. She's one of the only people who can soothe Aster when she goes off her meds.

Her meds.

I don't ask her if she took them. She doesn't need me reminding her of the only connection she has with her mother.

NINE

I don't want to go home. I want to stay with Josh, Maggie, and Stewart forever. But I miss Ivy. And I don't want to impose on this kind family. I make up the guest room after I wake, tucking the sheets in, shaking out the flowery comforter, and fluffing up the pillows until the bed looks pristine.

I take my backpack into the closest bathroom—Josh's. The mirror's still foggy from his shower, and the tiled walls smell citrusy like him. I fill my lungs with his soothing scent, let it envelop my skin like a silken robe.

I rub the fog off the mirror. My lids are puffy and my under-eye circles are almost purple, as though I've been punched. In a way, Mom's blame was a jab. A jab to the heart, not to the face, but emotions always leak into faces.

I hate her so much.

And yet, all that hatred has never funneled into the Machiavellian scheme I'm accused of. All I would have to do to have Mom taken away is show up in a hospital after one of our feuds. She stabbed my hand with a fork once. I still have four tiny, white scars under the knuckle of my right middle finger. She's locked me in the hallway closet more times than I care to remember. Once, she left me there the entire day. I ended up peeing myself, which won me name calling after she let me out.

I bet she bought the gun herself. To play the victim.

I need to find whom it's licensed to, that's what I need to do. Today.

I forgo a shower, but wash my face and tie my hair up. I dig through my backpack for my clothes—a white T-shirt and a pair of khaki drawstring shorts that I have to tighten so much they bunch unflatteringly around my waist. Thankfully, the T-shirt is long enough to hide the bunched effect.

I find my phone in the zippered pocket of my bag. It has six percent battery left, enough to read Ivy's many messages asking me how I am, how I feel, how sorry she is Mom took it out on me, how Mom's calmed down, how she's willing to apologize.

I can't forgive her, Ivy, I type back. ***Not this time. I'll come back, but I'll only come back for you. Not for her.***

Seconds later, Ivy texts me: ***You forgot your medication.***

I stare at her words.

I'm done taking drugs. It clouds my judgment. Besides, I don't really need it. I'm depressed sometimes, but it's because of Mom. If my home life was like Josh's, I wouldn't need to take happiness pills; I would simply be happy.

I turn off my phone and toss it back into my pack. When I get out of the bathroom, bag slung over my shoulder, I head downstairs but stop before reaching the landing. I hear Josh and his mom talking softly. He's telling her about last night. I hear the word gun.

"We have to call the authorities, Mom."

"They'll be eighteen in five months. If we call the police now, they might separate the girls, place them in worse homes."

No home can be worse than mine. They might be as terrible, though. Mom doesn't sexually abuse us, but what she does is also abuse.

"They might even send them to other towns, other states. They have one more year of high school. Uprooting them now would rattle their studies."

Why can't Josh's parents act as our legal guardians? I've never dared ask Josh or his mother because I didn't want to impose.

They stop talking so suddenly I worry they know I'm listening. I descend the last few steps to the landing. Maggie is grabbing her car keys and purse from a hook on the foyer wall.

She smiles at me, and I freeze in my tracks. Her kindness makes me regret eavesdropping. "Did you sleep well, honey?"

"Very well."

"I'm so glad to hear that. I have to get going, but Josh is in the kitchen." Right before leaving, she asks, "Want to help me make *sole à la normande* tonight?"

"Yes!" I hope my enthusiasm doesn't come off as desperation, but the thought of cooking, learning something new, is enthralling.

She chuckles. "Great. I'll see you later. Have a great day, hun."

When the door clicks shut, I head into the kitchen, where Josh is drinking tea. "Hey."

His eyes run over my face a mile a minute. He's trying to guess how I feel by my appearance. I look worse than I feel. "Mom let me off work today," he finally says.

"I need to buy something for Mr. Mancini." I twist my lips up. "I'm not sure what though. I kind of suck at guy gifts. Can you help me?"

He nods. For a while, the only noise comes from the AC vent blowing cool air over our heads. The tips of his short brown hair flutter.

"Aster?"

"Yeah."

"I ran the serial number of the gun last night on this website." His Adam's apple bobs in his freshly shaven throat. "The ATF—"

"The what?"

"It's an electronic tracing system for weapons."

"Oh."

"Anyway, the response came back a few minutes ago. It was bought in Noblesville at Gus's Guns." He pauses. Probably to give me a second to come to terms with the fact that Noblesville is the next town over. "I called them to find out if they were open, and they are. I was going to head there—"

"I'm coming with you."

"You don't have to."

"You don't want me to come with you?"

"I don't want to pressure you. You're under enough stress."

I smile to appease him. He worries about me too much. "I *want* to come with you."

He swallows, and his Adam's apple joggles again. "'Kay."

"Should we leave now?"

"I made you French toast."

"You...?" The rest of my words become suspended when I spot the plate of golden brown triangles.

Josh made me breakfast.

He cooked for me.

"Yeah. Mom supervised the whole thing though." He gestures toward the white marble dining table in the corner. It sits underneath an enormous silver lampshade that seems to have been salvaged from a ship. When I still haven't moved toward it, he says, "I ate some, and I didn't die, so you should be all right."

I laugh.

I walk over to the table and dig in, lifting large forkfuls into my mouth and chewing quickly, but savoring each morsel. I taste egg, maple syrup, and love. "Don't tell Maggie, but you might just cook better than her."

Josh joins me at the table with his tea. "Flatterer."

"Honest."

"Uh-huh." The intensity with which he observes me makes me blush. "I'm sorry I didn't believe you."

I shrug. "It's okay."

"No, it's not okay." His eyes are as green as moss this morning, and his brown hair gleams copper in the sunlight inundating the eat-in kitchen. "Ivy wanted you to call her."

I drop my gaze to my plate. "My phone died."

"You can use mine." He slides his cell toward me.

I eye it reluctantly. "I don't feel like calling her right now."

For a long moment, he stays silent, and I eat.

Everything vanishes from my plate into my mouth.

Josh cocks an eyebrow. "Are you mad at her for staying with your mother?"

"No. She needed to stay with Mom."

I take my plate to the sink and wash off the sticky remnants. My stomach burbles. I can't tell if I'm still hungry or if I ate too fast.

"You never told me how dinner went last night," Josh says.

I'm happy I have my back to him. "It went great."

"Really?"

I squeeze my eyes shut. "Yes." Even though my plate is clean, the water's still running. I'm afraid that if I turn off the tap, he'll hear my heightened pulse.

A hand settles gently on my shoulder and squeezes even more gently. In spite of the softness of Josh's touch, I jump. And then, I shiver. He doesn't raise his hand. He keeps it right on my sharp joint, bleeding delicious heat into my cold skin.

"Ivy told me you didn't order anything."

I don't answer, because if I do, he'll pity me, and that might change the way he's been looking at me since the dance.

The water stops gushing.

His other hand traps my free shoulder and spins me around slowly. "Aster?"

Slowly, I lift my lids. His tea-warmed breath tickles the tip of my nose. "I wasn't hungry last night."

He sighs, and it rumbles in the air between us. I lick my lips. His gaze drops to them, but then he releases me and turns away, his jaw pink.

TEN

JOSH

What am I doing? What the hell am I doing? I glance at Aster sitting in the passenger seat of my Camry. She's staring out the window. I sit up straighter. I've been having lots of indecent thoughts about her recently. She's starred in several dreams. I know it's her and not Ivy because the girl in my sleep has a small mole over her mouth like Aster. And Cindy Crawford. But the girl in those dreams was definitely not Cindy. Cindy does not have kinky blonde hair. Nor does she have lagoon-blue eyes.

I wonder if Aster knows how pretty she is.

My guess is no.

If she did, she wouldn't be hiding behind frumpy clothes.

She wouldn't be hanging out with me. The Hamster.

Sure, I'm not fat anymore, but she probably remembers me like that. And that memory must stain the way she sees me now.

She catches me gaping. Like a juvenile idiot, I blush.

Real men don't blush.

I try to think dampening thoughts. Mancini and his cat pop into my head. That cools me right down. It even propels a shudder down my spine. "You could get him a book about trees and flowers. He seems to like trees." He knew what type of tree grew in his backyard.

Old people like horticulture, don't they?

"Who's *him*?"

Right. "Mr. Mancini."

"That's a good idea. Maybe I can get him a landscaping book and a thriller. He has so many guns. I'm sure he likes thrillers."

"Good idea."

We drive the rest of the way in silence, both lost in our respective thoughts. I pump up the music and roll down my window. Sunny air licks my bare forearm, soothing after my crappy night. We arrive in Noblesville around lunchtime. The pavement wobbles from the humid heat.

I follow my phone's GPS to the firearm shop on 16th Street and park in the reserved lot.

As I click off my seatbelt, Aster asks, "What if it's stolen, Josh? Or what if it *was* used in a murder? Will they arrest us?"

I grab my nylon gym bag. I stuffed the gun in there this morning. "They wouldn't have any grounds for an arrest." That's a lie, though. We should've taken the gun to a police precinct. We shouldn't have kept it, much less driven around the state with it. I touch Aster's hand. It's stiff and feels as cold as the air spitting out of my AC. "It'll be all right, Asty. I promise."

Finally, she takes her seatbelt off and joins me on the other side of the car. Together we walk into the shop.

I suspect the owner is a big-game hunter. Every inch of the back wall is covered in rifles—from stainless synthetics to heavy wooden ones to automatics. But it's not as much the array of guns as the row of animal trophies—from heads to full bodies—cluttering the entrance. Even though the beasts are stuffed, their glassy eyes seem to follow us as we make our way to the glass counter that houses the handguns.

One other customer's in the shop. He's got his cap on backwards and his face is scruffy with a curly, red beard.

"Lydia!" the salesman showing him the rifles yells.

A woman scurries out the back, ruminating a wad of chewing gum. "Hiya. What can I help you kids with?"

"I ran an ATF trace on a gun in my possession, and the serial number matched a sale that came from this shop," I say.

"Come again? You have a gun but ran an ATF trace?"

"*Her* mom found a gun, and *I* ran a trace on it to figure where it came from."

The store's gotten awfully quiet.

"If it ain't yours, you need to take it to a precinct," Lydia says.

Aster shifts next to me.

"And we will," I say in a crisp voice, "but first, we were hoping you could tell us who you sold it to. That's all."

Lydia splays both her palms on the glass countertop. "Why?" The tips of her nails are sharpened to a point and lacquered purple. She could gouge someone's eye out with those.

"Because her mother isn't fit to carry a gun, so if she managed to procure herself one, she could probably procure herself more. And that's damnright frightening."

"Downright," Aster whispers.

"Huh?"

"Downright. Not damnright. Forget it," Aster mumbles.

"Did she threaten you with it, dear?" Lydia asks Aster.

Aster's bottom lip quivers. "She did."

"I'm sorry to hear that." The woman sighs, presses off the counter. "Can you kids show me some ID?"

I dig my driver's license out of my wallet and hand it over.

"I left mine in the car," Aster says. "I'll go get it. Josh, the keys?"

I give it to her, and she walks back through the forest of dead animals.

"Your girlfriend really got threatened by her mom?"

First instinct is to correct her—Aster isn't my girlfriend. She *is* my girl friend though. In the scope of things, it doesn't matter. "Yeah."

"Have you told the police?"

"Not yet."

"You better do it quick, son. I've seen these situations, and they can turn nasty. Sometimes fatal."

Silence fills the store. I shoot my gaze to the cap-wearing customer. He looks down fast and asks the salesman to see the lightest rifle they carry.

"Can I see the trace?" Lydia asks, dragging my attention back to her.

I dig the print-out from my bag, careful to keep the gun out of sight, and slap it on the counter. Blowing a humongous pink bubble, she picks up the printout, squints at the serial number, then enters it into the shop's computer.

Aster's back, driver's license in hand. "Here."

Lydia reaches for Aster's ID, glimpses at it, then whips her gaze back up toward us. Or more precisely, toward Aster.

I frown. "What?"

"The gun's in her name."

"What?" Aster cranes her neck to see the computer screen but it's one of those that's dark from an angle.

Color drains from my face. "*Her* name?" I pivot toward Aster. The wheels spin in my head, as fast as a gun barrel. And like a gun barrel, each chamber contains some harmful thought. "It's registered to you?"

"To another Aster. Not to me." Beads of perspiration form on her small nose. That happens when she's frightened or when she's stressed out.

Which is it at that moment? Fear or anxiety?

ELEVEN

J osh gapes at me in a way that makes the hair on my arms rise. He thinks I bought the gun. Tears scald my eyes. I don't blink because I don't want them to drip out. Instead, I tilt my face toward the beige popcorn ceiling so the tears slide back in.

Lydia smacks the gum around in her mouth. "Well it says here the gun's registered to Aster—"

"Lydia!" the rifle salesman says sharply. "That's enough."

It startles her so much that she swallows her gum and starts coughing.

"I'll take over from here. You take care of Mr. Conrath." He stalks over to us. "Do you have the gun with you?"

"No."

I gape at Josh. He never lies! It's a great sin in his family. It's even worse than cursing.

"We're not stupid enough to drive around with a stolen weapon," Josh adds.

"Where is it?"

"I locked it up in my parents' safe."

I study my brown, too-small sandals. I'm not a good liar. I'm not even a good co-liar. If the salesman checks my face, he'll understand Josh is being deceitful.

"Then I can't help you."

"Super customer service you guys got here," Josh says.

"We respect our customers' privacy"—he glares at Lydia, who starts wheezing. Maybe the gum got stuck in her airway —"so yeah, I agree, we provide excellent service, young man. Now, if you please. We have *actual* customers who need our help."

Josh and the salesman have a staring competition while Lydia chugs a bottle of water in great, wet gulps.

"Do the last names match?" Josh tries.

"Look, kid, I remember who bought the gun, and it wasn't her."

Knuckles whitening around the handle of his nylon bag, Josh swipes our IDs off the countertop and springs out of the shop. I rush out after him.

He waits for me by the car. I walk to the passenger side and tug on my door handle but it's still locked.

"You have the keys, Aster."

I pat my back pocket. Find the mini dumbbell keychain. I beep the Camry open, then get in and drop the keys in the drink holder, next to a half-eaten tube of Mentos.

He twists the key in the ignition but doesn't move the

gearshift out of park. His eyes are closed and his nostrils flare. He must be trying to calm down. "Did you have someone buy it?"

"What?"

"The gun, Aster. It was in your name. Did you ask someone to buy it for you?"

My molars grind at his harsh accusation. I lock my arms in front of my pulsating chest and angle my body away from his.

"Aster." He tries to touch my arm, but I shift away before his hand can settle.

"I can't believe you would think that." My voice sounds flimsy, weak...like me.

"The gun's registered in your—"

"It's registered to someone called Aster!" I shake my head.

He drags his hands through his hair and pulls at the roots. His biceps bulge in his Metallica T-shirt.

"I'm not the only person named Aster in this world," I add, although I shouldn't have to.

He sighs, releases his hair. "You think your mom used your name to buy it?"

"I. Don't. Know."

Tension and regret writhe within his jade irises. "I'm sorry." Josh cups my cheeks. Makes me look at him. "Please forgive me."

I swallow hard. "You hurt me."

He presses his forehead against mine. "I'm so sorry." His words vibrate against my nose. With his thumbs, he whisks away my tears. "I hate myself right now."

"You know I could never stay mad at you, but you—"

He hushes me with a brush of his finger against my lips.

A shiver shoots all the way down my throat and creates concentric ripples inside my heaving chest. "...hurt me." I'm surprised I manage to finish my sentence when Josh's mouth is so close to mine. If I tilt my head up, our lips will meet.

I don't move, though, because his accusation pulses inside my mind like a bee sting.

I slide my face out of his warm palms. The air vents cool my cheeks. "Why did you lie about having the gun?"

"Because they would've taken it away from us." He studies his gear shift. "And I'm holding out hope that the police can tell us who this...*other* Aster is."

<hr>

AFTER JOSH DROPS me off on my street, I cross the road and ring Mr. Mancini's doorbell. He comes outside in a pair of olive-green cargo shorts and a black T-shirt that has several small holes along the collar and in the hem. Perhaps I should've gotten him mothballs instead of books.

He stares at me without saying a word, his eyes swollen and pink like rosebuds.

"I got you this. It won't bring Bullet back, but it might help ease your pain." I hand him my gift-wrapped present.

He doesn't take it from me. He must hate me. Hate my entreaty. I'm so ashamed I drop my gaze to his doormat that reads: *The neighbors have better stuff*. I doubt he picked it. He doesn't strike me as humorous. Plus, on this street, no one has better stuff.

When he still doesn't take the gift from me, I crouch and place it on the word *neighbors* and flee. He's still standing outside, motionless, when I let myself inside my house.

I've decided to confront my mother.

Her studio door is closed. A husky man's voice trickles out through the thin wood door. I listen, wondering if Mom has company. It's been a long time since she's brought home a man.

The voice takes a high-pitched tone.

Audiobook.

I knock softly. "Mom?"

The sound shuts off with a click.

I try the doorknob but it's locked.

Footsteps resound on the other side.

The door creaks open.

Mom's haggard eyes fix on me. "What?"

I jerk backward from the crispness of her voice. "You registered the gun in my name."

Her pupils pulse against their light backdrop. We have the same eye color, except hers is a crueler shade than mine. "Are you testing my patience?"

The key she wears around her neck swings against her shapeless white blouse. It's the key to all her secrets. Sometimes, I think it's the key to her heart, but then I remember she doesn't have one.

"The gun was registered to Aster. Why did you put my name—"

"I didn't buy a gun!" She jabs her index finger against my collarbone repeatedly. "Are you thick?"

I jerk backward.

"Have you called child services yet?" she asks, breathing hard.

"What?"

She slaps her forehead. "Of course you didn't. You're not eighteen yet." She gives me an ugly smile full of pretty teeth. "I'm not a perfect mother, Aster, but you're not a perfect daughter either."

I recoil.

"Thank God we have Ivy," she says.

I try to peek behind her to see if my sister's there, but the gap's not wide enough. And it's getting narrower. I place my palm on the door to keep it open so that my last words can penetrate. "You are so mean."

She snorts softly. "The world's a mean place, Aster. Get that through your head. Everything it gives, it takes back. You're not too young to understand that. Learn it. It'll hurt less." And then she shuts the door in my face.

The air whooshes against me.

I'm too shocked to cry.

On autopilot, I walk toward my bedroom and grab clean clothes because there's no way in hell I'm staying in this goddamn house. After I repack my backpack, I write Ivy a note to tell her I'm okay, that I'm going back to see Josh, and that I love her. I text Josh to tell him I'm ready. He answers right back: ***Still at the precinct. Be there in fifteen.***

Since I don't want to breathe the same tainted air as my mother, I sit on our front stoop to wait.

I look up at the stars twinkling in the purpling sky and wonder what my father could've seen in my mother. I bet she was nice with him at first, and then, when he saw her true face, it drove him away. Even though she loves to tell us it was her pregnancy that made him run. I think she's lying. I think Dad wanted us. Who wouldn't want innocent babies?

As I take in my sleepy neighborhood, I stroke my abdomen and think of baby Violet.

A dog barks in someone's backyard.

Will my daughter like dogs?

Simmering tomato sauce and sautéed onions flavor the dusky air.

Will she enjoy my cooking?

A TV blares from a living room.

A cartoon.

Headlights from a shiny Jeep splash the low hedge lining our front yard and then Mr. Mancini's doormat.

My present is no longer there.

TWELVE

JOSH

"Can I subpoena information from a store?" I ask Jackie, dropping into the chair across from her desk at the precinct.

"Come again?"

At this hour, the precinct is almost empty.

"Say someone bought something, and to buy it, that person needed to give some personal information, can I subpoena that information?"

Her penciled-in eyebrows shoot upward. "Have you been accused of something, Josh?"

"No! Why would you think that?"

"Because subpoenas are used in court cases."

I lock my fingers together, lean forward, balancing my forearms on my thighs. "I'm not facing any accusations or anything."

"Then why are you talking about subpoenas?"

"I just thought..." My shoulders tense up. "I just thought I could compel someone to give me information legally."

"What information do you need?"

"I can't tell you."

"Josh, you're scaring me, and I'm a cop. I'm tough to scare. What information do you need?"

I chew on my bottom lip. I can tell her? Right? But then, this tiny part of me yells, *What if Aster bought the gun?* Even Jackie won't be able to protect her then. "Forget it. I'll look it up online."

"You know you can trust me."

I nod as I get up.

"If this was dangerous, you'd tell me, right?"

My jaw prickles. "Yes," I lie.

She stares into my face a good, long while. "You're a good kid, Josh, but a bad liar."

She's right. I suck at lying.

ON WHITEPAGES.COM, I look up people with the name Aster. I'm not sure whether I'm supposed to be looking at last names or first names. I add Indiana in the location tab. Only seven Asters left, including Aster Redd.

I start calling the numbers listed below the names. I don't start by asking if they have a license to carry. I ask if they know a woman named Rose Redd. The first guy I phone asks me if this is a prank call. I tell him, *no. Rose Redd?* he repeats incredulously. *Yeah, Rose Redd,* I repeat abrasively.

Even though I'm not the one who picked Mrs. Redd's first name, I take his mocking tone personally.

"Nope," he says. "Don't know any Roses."

I try the next ones. Call each of them up. Two don't

answer, so I leave voicemails, and the two others have never heard of a Rose Redd, or been to Noblesville *or* Kokomo.

The following day, I call the two who didn't answer. This time I reach one of them. A woman. Rachel Aster. A ninety-seven-year old nursing home resident. She apologizes for not returning my call, but a rectal exam had her feeling woozy. I grimace, tell her I'm sorry for her pain, I hope she recovers quickly. There's no recovery at her age for colon cancer, but heck, because her cells are so old, the disease is spreading slowly. Doctor told her it could be months before she dies. I pace around my bedroom as she tells me about how her grandkids don't come visit often and asks if I visit my grandparents often. I spent a week in April with them. And I'm planning another trip soon. And then they're coming up here for Thanksgiving, and—

And then I stop talking. I'm supposed to be finding the owner of a gun, not discussing my family relationships with a complete—albeit friendly—stranger.

Unable to hang up on someone, I keep talking to Rachel for another *fifteen minutes* until she finally tells me she's late for her game of euchre. Before disconnecting, she makes me swear to call my grandmother today. Never know if they'll be there tomorrow. I promise I will.

I take a breather after that. Go eat two bananas. Chug down a diet Red Bull.

A half hour later, I try the last Aster again. The only other Aster who carries the name as a first name: Aster Colson.

She doesn't answer so I text her, Hi. My name is Joshua Cooper. Do you know a woman named Rose Redd?

I type the name in Google. Find out Aster Colson owns a security firm in Indiana. I click on the Bio tab of the webpage. A picture of a man with a shaved head, light brown skin, and a thick neck materializes on my monitor. I know it's stupid, but the fact that he's a man stuns me more than the fact he's ex-military.

Soft rasping at my bedroom door startles me.

I shut down my browser. "Who is it?"

"It's Aster." She cracks the door open. "They want me to come back tomorrow. They liked me." She was filling in for a waitress at the old diner on Fulham Street.

I rub the heels of my hands into my eyes. "That's great."

"Yeah. I made all of eighteen dollars in tips today. I can almost take you to a movie tonight."

"Take me? *I* do the taking." Her reddening cheeks make me realize how it sounds. Like I'm asking her on a date. My palms are moist, so I rub them against my pant legs. "Want to go to a movie with me tonight?"

Her gaze drops to my beige carpet that's whiter in spots where I used bleach to get dirt stains out. I thought Mom would applaud my initiative, but I ended up damaging it instead of fixing it. Although proud of me, she advised me to check with her next time I felt like housekeeping.

"Sure. Should we—" Aster fingers a little hole in her black leggings. "Should I ask Ivy too?"

"No." I whip the word out way too fast. Desperate much? I'm tempted to slap my forehead but clutch the chair's armrests instead. "I want to make it up to you. You know"—I shrug—"because of my assumption yesterday."

Her mouth bursts apart with the softest gasp. Maybe I shouldn't have reminded her. Maybe she's already put it past her.

"*We're the Millers* looks good," she suggests.

"Yeah it does. Let me see what time it's playing."

I check the local movie theater for showings.

"Did you find anything?" She sits cross-legged on my bed and tips her pointy chin toward my monitor.

"It's playing at seven-thirty."

"I meant about *Aster?*"

I'm tempted to show her Colson's picture. Ask her if she's ever seen him. For some reason, I shake my head.

She sighs. "Maybe we should go back to the gun shop. Maybe if we give them the gun, they'll give us the person's full name."

"What if it's *your* full name?"

"Then we'll know for sure it was Mom who bought it." She taps the floor with the rubber sole of her Converse. "The police really ran the serial number and found nothing?"

"Yeah. They got directed to the same website where I ran the ATF trace."

Aster thinks I showed Jackie the gun because that's what I told her. But if I'd shown it to Jackie, and she'd traced it back to Aster...*my* Aster— I shudder just thinking about it.

Even though Aster blames her mother, a tiny part of me still wonders if Aster commissioned someone to buy it for her. She doesn't have many friends—just me really—but she told me she met a girl in her shrink's waiting room. A girl with hairy legs and a nose piercing who never speaks. What if it's a lie though? What if she *does* speak? What if they've had conversations? About guns, for example?

Aster stretches her neck to the side. It cracks. "You'd think the police would have their own database."

"You'd think."

"Explains why gun control is so crappy in this country."

"Yeah."

She sighs. "My feet are killing me, and I smell like stale fries. I'm going to go shower and lie down for a bit." She rises from my bed, but pauses in my doorway. "We are going to the movies, right?"

"Yeah. I mean, if you want to."

Her eyes linger on mine. "I want to."

A small current passes between us, zaps me, zips up my spine, stiffens my neck. We've gone to the movies together hundreds of times, so why does this time feel different?

I spend a long time in front of the mirror, attempting to smooth my curls with the coconut butter I found in the Coopers' pantry. It's greasy, but it makes my hair shiny and gives it an exotic smell, as though I've frolicked on a sandy beach full of sunshine. I twist in front of the mirror, my glossy locks clumping together. I probably put on an insane amount, but it's too late to take a shower and shampoo it out.

If only Ivy helped me. She's so good at all this. But I haven't even called my sister today, and she hasn't called me either.

I finger-comb my hair some more, then screw the lid back on the glass jar of the nut butter and exit the bathroom, hiding the tub underneath the uneven hem of my T-shirt. It wasn't always uneven, but Ivy did the laundry once and hung it to dry with a clip, which stretched out the fabric. It's not unwearable, but then again, what do I know of fashion?

Maybe I look awful. I wish I could ask Ivy...

I'm about to go downstairs when I hear Josh talking with his parents. I double back to my room and stuff the glass jar underneath my pillow. Then I head down, trying to push out the nervousness fueling the thunderous pounding of my heart.

"I'm ready to go."

All three Coopers stare at me.

"Don't you look pretty tonight," Josh's father tells me.

"And you smell so good," adds Maggie, sniffing the air. "Like coconut. Hmm. That gives me an idea for a pound cake."

"Honey," Stewart says, "you're off work."

She leans over the table and pecks his lips. "You're never off work when you work for yourself."

"*I* work for myself."

"And the Discolis."

The shells of his ears glow bright red. "They hired me."

"I was teasing you. My work is just so much more fun than yours." Maggie leans over, but before she can place another kiss on her husband's lips, Josh's voice halts her.

"Guys, I'm right here."

Maggie grins wickedly. "Aren't the people who made you allowed to express their love for each other?"

"Yeah, but in private. Yeesh." Josh rolls his eyes.

If there ever was an ideal couple, the Coopers are it. Perfect and loving and responsible. They never left their five-year-old behind at home while they ran errands. They never told him how inconvenient his birth was to their career. They never used cruelty to harden him.

"We gotta go. Movie starts in fifteen." Even though Josh

complains about his parents' PDA, I don't think he actually minds it.

"I love your parents," I tell him as we make our way out to his car.

His hands are stuffed in his track pants. "Yeah. I got lucky."

"I want what they have."

He glances at me. "What? You don't want what *your* parents had?"

"That's a paltry joke, Josh."

"Paltry?"

"Mean."

"Yeah. I'm sorry."

As he starts driving, he repeats the word *paltry* a couple times. That's how he teaches himself things. He has to say them a couple times, and then they're cemented in him. I usually only need to read or hear something once to learn it.

"I'm sorry, Asty. That was really *poultry* of me."

My mouth splits into a smile. "Paltry with an A. Not poultry."

He clucks, then winks. "I know. Just wanted to see you smile."

WE FIND seats easily in the nearly empty theater. A large bucket of popcorn rests on my lap. Every now and again, Josh's hand sneaks into the bucket, and like one of his dad's diggers, scoops popcorn out.

The trailers begin. I love trailers. I like anything that's exciting and forthcoming. It's not that I don't appreciate the present—like right now, sitting in a dark movie theater with the boy I've had a crush on for ten years: that's pretty amazing—but I live for the future. I know it'll be better, because it can't possibly be worse.

My hand collides with Josh's in the popcorn bucket.

He doesn't pull his hand out, even though his fingers aren't ploughing through the puffy kernels. Something must be distracting him.

My gaze climbs up to his.

He's staring straight back.

The bright glow of the screen makes his eyes sparkle like black emeralds shimmering in a forgotten pirate chest. Before I can ask him why he's looking at me, his hand arcs out of the bucket and settles on the nape of my neck. Grains of salt transfer from his palm to my skin.

Without hesitation, he brings his lips down on mine, and stars shoot around me. His mouth is soft and warm and tastes like salt and butter. His tongue, though, is not soft. It prods my lips open and slides in, seeking my own tongue hungrily.

I've been holding out for this kiss forever, and yet, instead of reciprocating, I become stiller than a mummy. And then the moment is over, and Josh is saying, "I'm sorry," but I'm the one who's sorry.

If I don't reach out now, if I don't bridge the space between our faces, if I don't let him know that kissing me is fine, better than fine, he will never do it again, and I can't live in a world where Josh doesn't kiss me anymore.

I lay a hand on the hot band of skin above his T-shirt collar and pull him to me. And then, breaking out of my tight, hard shell, *I kiss him. I* touch my tongue to his. *I* knock my teeth into his.

This time, he's the one who doesn't respond, yet I keep stroking his tongue, his teeth, his lips, because I want a reaction.

I *need* a reaction.

I press my mouth against his harder, crush my fingertips into his skin, then rub them gently over the downward peak of silky, shorn hair that dips toward his spine.

Finally, as though I've found the correct combination, he comes alive and reacts with more heat and tenderness than I could ever have wished for.

FOURTEEN

JOSH

I hold Aster's hand tight throughout the whole movie. And I kiss her again.

My heart is scrambling to beat normally. *That girl*. I don't know what it is about her, besides the fact that she's hot, but I'm so attracted to her. Maybe it's the way she makes me feel: needed. Or maybe it's our shared past.

After the movie is over—a movie that I'll have to watch again because I have no clue what went down—we're still kissing. The lights are bright now, and the room is almost empty. Two staff members walk in with brooms and standing dustpans.

I shift away from Aster, let go of her hand. Her cheeks are flushed and her mouth is taillight-red. She stands and waits for me to stand too, but I need to readjust myself before I rise. I don't want her to notice the bulge in my jeans.

I focus on the cleaning crew to quiet down.

It takes a couple seconds but it works. I stand up and walk behind Aster, my gaze drifting from the ends of her hair to the dimples in her lower back that peek out of her lopsided T-shirt.

I ask if she wants to grab a kebab at the Turkish place next door. It's crowded, so we get ours to go and walk through the flowery alleys of Highland Park. When we reach the deserted playground, Aster sits on a red plastic swing. She's still eating her kebab, while I've finished mine and balled the aluminum foil. I toss it into a bin, pretending it's a free throw. My aluminum missile sinks right into the center of the bin.

Swinging gently, Aster seals the aluminum edges around her kebab and lays it in the sand at her feet.

I latch on to the chains of her swing and steady her. Her giant blue eyes climb up to my face. A tiny glob of tahini is stuck to her upper lip, right next to her mole. I lean down and lick it off.

And then I'm kissing her again.

I tug her up, take her seat on the swing, then pull her down onto my lap.

Slowly, I dig my sneaks into the ground and push, giving the swing momentum.

"You think Ivy"—Aster swallows—"you think she'll mind that we...we...?"

"Made out?" I finish for her. "Why would Ivy mind?"

"She might find it weird."

"So what? We don't need her permission." Her hair curtains off half her face, yet I still see her reddened cheeks. "We don't need anyone's permission." I tuck the wall of hair behind her ear, but it springs back out. I gather it in my hand, all of her hair, and twist it away, and then I apply light pressure to the back of her head to bring her face closer to mine. "Kiss me again."

Her mouth curves into a dazzling smile that floods her eyes. They shine, brighter than the moon overhead.

Aster isn't my first kiss, but she's the first girl I've kissed whom I know inside out.

She blinks and a tear tumbles down her cheek.

My heart holds still. "Are you crying?"

She nods.

"Why?"

"Because...I didn't think you felt the same way I did."

"Aster Redd...I—" I'm about to say the L-word, but that'll scare her. It scares me. "I've *always* liked you."

She sniffles. Smiles. But she's still crying.

"Don't cry." She's always been sensitive, but she seems especially emotional tonight. I can't help but wonder if she's taking her mood stabilizers. Then again, she's a girl, and girls are emotional. "I don't want you to cry every time I kiss you," I say softly.

"Every time?"

"You didn't think this was a one-off, did you?"

More tears traipse down. I let go of her hair to whisk the wetness off her cheeks with my thumbs, and then I kiss her forehead and pull her close, until her head is resting in the crook of my neck.

"Aster Redd, if it's okay with you, I'd like to kiss you every day from now on."

She sniffs again. "You don't have to ask permission."

"Men should always ask a woman's permission to kiss them."

She grins, then whispers, "Okay. You have my permission."

TONIGHT IS one of those times I wished I weren't living with my parents anymore, but it makes no financial sense to pay for room and board when I live a couple miles from campus.

Holding onto Aster's hand, I lead her up the stairs of my quiet house—Mom and Dad always go to bed early. I should probably part ways with her in front of the guest bedroom, but I don't.

I sit down on the bed and pat the spot next to me. She lowers herself, as stiff as a knitting needle.

"I don't want to have sex with you," I blurt out, so she'll relax.

She blinks, lets out a soft gasp. "You don't?"

"Tonight. I mean, tonight. I didn't take you in here to… you know, take advantage of you"—I rub the nape of my neck—"or anything."

Whoa. I sound like such a loser. I squeeze my eyes shut and massage them with my balled fingers, wishing I could rub the stupidity right out of me. Aster scoots closer to me, her sharp hipbone digging into my thigh. "As long as you want to make love to me someday, then I'm okay with waiting."

Wait, *what?* Did I just ask her to wait for me? I don't want to wait. I haven't had any action in months. I'm more than willing and ready to go. I'm about to tell her all of that— well, except the part where I haven't had sex in so long—but I bite my tongue.

Literally, I bite it.

This is Aster. Not some random girl I picked up next to a beer keg at a frat house party.

I want our first time to be special.

Before I can make more of a fool of myself, she lays one hand on my jaw and nudges my mouth open with hers. And then she's straddling me, and I fall backward on the bed. My breath rips right out of me for two reasons.

One, that was hot. Her taking charge.

Two, my head hits something hard that's not the headboard. I reach beneath the pillow and pull out a glass jar.

"Coconut butter," I read out loud. "Why do you have coconut butter under your pillow?" Aster is a messy person, but food—well not food, a condiment—in bed is a bit weird, even for her.

"I tossed it there before leaving. It must've rolled underneath the pillow." She's so flustered, her words tumble out and her face floods with color.

Smiling, I place it on the nightstand, brush away the black leggings that hang half on half off the comforter, then pull her against me and remind her of what we were doing. She's gone stiff again, and it takes my hands running up and down her spine several times to loosen her, to make her forget about the interruption.

My phone vibrates in my jeans. I don't want to stop, but I yank my phone out of my pocket. I'm about to pitch it onto the nightstand when I read the text message: **Never heard of Rose.**

Aster Colson's finally answered me. *Great timing, dude.*

Aster slides off me. "Who's that?"

Instead of lying, I tell her about my furtive investigation, about my lead. I look for disappointment in her eyes but find none. She's not mad. But our conversation has definitely killed the mood. She's thinking about the gun.

"You think my mother knows—*knew*—another Aster than myself?" she asks.

I pull her against me, kiss her forehead. "It's possible, right? I mean, you're not the only one with the name."

But it would be quite the coincidence.

A pretty major coincidence.

The wheels spin inside my head so hard and fast I'm afraid an actual grating sound is coming from my ears.

To show Jackie, or not to show her?

To return to the gun shop, or not to return?

"How's that friend of yours from the doctor's office? You know the girl with the hairy legs?" I murmur into Aster's coconut-y curls, hoping it can spur a memory...or a confession.

She doesn't answer me. I press her lightly away so I can see her face.

She's fast asleep.

FIFTEEN

After

The day after Josh and I start dating, I return home.

I do it for Ivy.

She took the bus over to Josh's house. Told me that Mom's psychiatrist readjusted her meds. That Mom is doing better. Has become calmer.

"She woke up asking if you'd died," Ivy tells me as I drive us to a place that should feel like home but doesn't.

Home has never been a place.

Home has always been people.

Home is Ivy and Josh.

Ivy is the hearth that warms the walls my arms form around us, and Josh is our roof, our floor, the one who keeps us sheltered and grounded.

"Asking or hoping?" I ask.

"What?" Ivy's hair is twisted into a bun atop her head and wrapped with a piece of gold silk that matches her hair color. The sun always burnishes her hair in the summer. I don't like to sit in direct sunlight, but Ivy does. She takes real pleasure in laying out.

"Nothing."

I take a right on our street. Although a great rainstorm washed over Kokomo this morning, blowing rubbery leaves off thick branches, gluing them to car windshields, our driveway still seems blemished with Bullet's ruby-black blood. The stain is in my mind, indelible, however much rain falls over my town and over my body.

"How's Mr. Mancini?" I glance over at his front door.

"Haven't seen him."

"I'll go visit him later. Want to come?"

"Sure."

I turn the car off, but stay inside.

"Asty, Mom loves you. In her own way." Ivy clasps my hand in hers. "She would never *hope* for your death."

So my sister did hear me.

"Besides, I forbid you to leave me. What would I do without my better half?"

My eyes heat up. "I *did* leave you. The moment things got hard, I left."

"Asty, I'm not mad at you for going with Josh. You needed space to process all that happened, and so did Mom." Ivy bites her lip. "Can I ask you something, though? Mom mentioned that the last time you talked, you asked her about someone called Aster?"

"I wasn't asking about myself, if that's your question."

Ivy studies the mold-speckled wall of our apartment building through the windshield. "You didn't take your medication with you to Josh's."

I yank my hand out of hers. "You all believe my world will start spinning out of control if I stop gulping down my pills, but all they do is numb me. Make Mom's abuse sufferable. Make the world a little shinier."

Ivy's copper skin pales.

"The gun's registered to an *Aster*, and that Aster isn't me. Josh asked Jackie to run the serial number through the police database." I lie because I want Ivy to stop looking at me like I'm some sad lost puppy. "I'll bet you anything Mom stashed that gun in her drawer and has been keeping it there."

Ivy's mouth slackens.

"You said you saw rolls of fabric in there. Who locks up fabric? Want to know what I think? I think she hid the gun inside the rolls of fabric."

Ivy sucks in a breath. "You think?"

"Why would she lock up fabric?"

My twin's gaze shifts downward. Is there something she's not telling me?

Perhaps there's no fabric at all in the drawer.

Perhaps my sister lied to me.

I study her hooded eyes and pressed lips in silence. "Show me what's inside."

Her eyes sweep up to mine. "You don't believe me?"

"Do you ever believe *me*?"

She clicks her seatbelt off and pushes the door open. "I've just been through hell with Mom. Don't you put me through hell too." She gets out and shuts the door.

Reluctantly, I step out of the car and follow her. "You're turning this around."

She spins on her wedge sneakers, throws her hands in the air. "You turned it around first!"

All I want is a glimpse into Mom's damn drawer. If she

isn't hiding anything, why am I not allowed a peek? "I'm sorry. I believe you."

After a moment, she says, "Okay," and walks into the house. I wonder if I should've told her about Josh. He's her friend too after all. But part of me is keeping this secret tucked away. What if she's against our relationship? What if she's disgusted? Josh and I are close, almost like siblings.

Or worse...

What if she's jealous? Has she ever thought of Josh that way?

I double back to the Honda and pop the trunk open to grab my backpack. As I hoist it out, a forest-green Jeep parks in front of Mancini's house.

Did he buy a new car? No one comes out. I squint to make out the driver, but the glass is tinted. Maybe it's his daughter. Maybe she heard about his loss and came down for a visit. Or up. I'm not sure where she lives.

"Aster?" Ivy calls out. She stands in the open doorway of our house. "Are you coming?"

"Yeah." I shut the trunk of my car and brace myself to enter the place I hate above all others, to see the person I fear above all others.

SIXTEEN

JOSH

It's been a week since I kissed Aster. A week since she kissed me back. A week during which we've kissed a lot. But never in public. At least not in front of people we know like my parents, Ivy, or my college buddies. Neither of us have told anyone about what we're doing. When I ask Aster if it bothers her, she says no. She likes keeping things to herself. Frankly, so do I.

As I wait in front of her school with a foil-wrapped BLT from the deli—Aster's favorite sandwich—I text Jackie to tell her I'll be a little late. I asked her to meet me at Mom's bakery. I didn't tell her why I wanted to see her. Just that it has to do with my visit to the precinct the other day and my question about subpoenas. I've decided to tell her about the gun. She'll know what to do.

I spot Ivy first. She's walking arm-in-arm with Felicity Suell. I feel a pang of dismay that she's friends with Felicity.

I know for a fact that the chick bullied Aster back in middle school. Granted, people change, but Felicity, with her high-pitched giggles and dramatic hair flipping, acts exactly the same as she did back then. She lost the braces but not the attitude.

The second Ivy notices me, she walks over. "Hey!"

"Good first day?"

"Yeah. Best ever."

I arch an eyebrow. "*Best ever?*"

"I'm a senior. This is the beginning of the end."

"And there's a party at my house this weekend," Felicity shoots in. "Wanna join, Josh? We'd love to have some real men around." Her hand skims over my bicep. "Plus, you could bring some of your friends. Preferably of the male gender."

I shrug her off. "Is Aster going?"

Ivy scrunches her nose. "Probably not."

"Is she invited?" I ask her, but it's Felicity who answers.

"Whole senior class is invited. I'm even letting some juniors in on the fun. I have a *big* house. But you know that."

Felicity's mansion is the second largest estate in Kokomo after the Discolis'. While the latter live in a palace surrounded by a moat and castle-worthy gardens, the Suells own four acres of land with a private tennis court and a grotto-style outdoor pool.

I hooked up with Felicity's French cousin in that pool.

Aster chooses that moment to pop out of the school doors. I shove the memory as far away as I can. I shouldn't be thinking about other girls. The second her gaze alights upon me, her tense features smooth out and she smiles. But then she sees Felicity, and Aster's face falls a little. Cautiously she approaches us, fingers wrapped tight around her backpack straps.

"We were just talking to Josh about the party at my house this weekend," Felicity tells her. "Anyway, I gotta go. I have cheerleading practice in twenty minutes. You should totally try out, Ivy. I've seen you dance. You've got moves, girl."

Ivy blushes and smiles. Felicity smacks a kiss on Ivy's cheek, then starts leaving but spins around. "FYI, Manon will be there, Josh. Apparently schools in France don't start for another two weeks." She winks and leaves, putting me in a really uncomfortable situation.

"Was that the girl you had sex with in Felicity's pool?" Ivy asks.

I tug on the neck of my wife-beater that seems made out of chainmail. "I didn't have sex with her."

Aster's studying her brown sandals. Her toes poke out over the sole.

"Sorry. *You made out with*," Ivy says, emphasizing each word.

I jerk my head back up. "Can we not discuss my exes?"

Ivy's eyebrows slant on her forehead.

Aster still hasn't looked up, which is starting to worry me.

I offer her the foil-wrapped sandwich. "I got you a BLT."

She raises her head. Relaxes the death grip she's exerting on her backpack. She still doesn't take my offering though.

I pluck her hand off the strap and place the ball of warm foil inside her palm. I keep my hand on hers, hoping it will get her thinking about something other than my hook-up with Felicity's cousin. Hoping it will remind her that Manon means nothing to me. Nothing compared to what *she*—Aster Redd—means to me.

"Asty, you don't need to go to this party," Ivy tells her, misunderstanding her sister's sudden tension.

Aster smiles at her twin. "I know. I might have to work on Friday anyway…"

Ivy smiles back, and then becomes distracted. "Hold on a sec. I just want to ask Stephanie if she managed to switch into my AP Math class." Ivy trots over to a girl with auburn hair and a mask of freckles that gives the impression she's always tanned.

"Are *you* going to the party?" Aster asks me.

"I'd rather take you out to dinner. Unless you really are working."

Patches of flushed skin burn on her cheeks and neck. For a moment, she looks like one of her mother's quilts, made of various silks and cottons and threads. "I'd rather have dinner with you."

My heart thumps as we gaze at each other in silence. "BLT's still warm," I remind her.

Her crystal-clear eyes drop to the forgotten ball of foil in her hand. She unwraps it as though it were some delicately packaged present, and then she lifts it to her mouth and takes a large bite. I watch her lips move. When her tongue darts out to lick her lips, a ton of fantasies spiral through my mind.

Most of them do not involve a sandwich.

Most of them involve her and me and darkness. Semi-darkness. Not total darkness. I want to see her body, not simply feel it. I want to see those transparent eyes of hers rake me in while the rest of her takes me in.

Whoa.

Dinner.

It's only dinner.

From the corner of my eye, I spy Ivy heading back our way. I plunk my hands into my sweatpants' pockets and push the fabric out so she doesn't notice the effect my dirty mind just had on my body.

"Can we stop by Goodwill on our way home?" Ivy asks. "I want to see if I can dig up something to wear to the party."

Aster nods. "Want half my sandwich?"

"You're not hungry anymore?" Ivy asks.

Aster shakes her head, so her twin snatches the sandwich and scarfs it down. The girl can eat. I'm pretty sure she eats more than me. But she's never had weight problems.

"I should get going. I have a meeting with a study group in twenty at the campus library."

"Thanks for coming," Aster says, her voice as soft as the flower she was named after.

"About that, why *are* you here? Not that I'm not happy to see you," Ivy says.

"Just wanted to check up on my two favorite girls."

Ivy grins. "No wonder you can't find a girlfriend. Who'd want to be third best? Actually fourth best. Maggie's third, right?"

"Maybe I have a girlfriend," I interject.

Ivy's eyes become as wide as the rims on my car. "That you haven't told us about?"

Shoot. I glance over at Aster for help, even though I'm not sure how she can dig me out of the hole I flung myself into. "I said *maybe*," I mumble.

"I think I'm being followed," Aster says suddenly, gaze on the parking lot beyond me.

"What?" Ivy blurts out, shielding her eyes to see the object of her twin's attention.

"What makes you think that?" I ask, spinning to scan the rows of cars.

"The forest-green Jeep over there. It was in front of our house last week. Well, in front of Mr. Mancini's house. And it was also in front of the diner when I got off my shift a couple days ago."

"Are you sure?" I ask, adrenaline spiking through my veins.

She nods.

Without a second thought, I take off toward the parked Jeep.

"Josh, stop!" Ivy yells. "Come on. Let's not do anything brash—"

I don't stop.

A hand wraps around my forearm, tugs me back. The manicured nails tell me it's Ivy. Aster never polishes her nails. "Slow down a sec."

Aster hasn't moved. She's still standing in the spot where we left her.

"Why would anyone be following her?" Ivy asks in a hushed voice.

"Because of the gun."

"How would they even know she has it? And how the heck would they know where she lives?"

"We took the gun to the shop where it was purchased. We had to show them some ID."

Ivy chews on her lip. Her fingers loosen on my arm but stay put. "Okay. So there's an actual possibility that my sister's *not* being paranoid...?" Ivy half-asks, half-states.

I hadn't even considered this. I think back on the time she was certain one of her mother's exes was trying to kill her. She hadn't reacted when he'd choked on a piece of meat—neither had she performed the Heimlich maneuver nor had she phoned 9-1-1—which had led him to call her a psychopath. Which in turn had led her mother to shake her so hard, it had left bruises on her upper arms.

By the time she told me the story, the *asshole*—God knows I don't use curse words lightly—had left, and so had the twins' mother, who'd gone after him to salvage their effed-up relationship.

Again, the twins had stayed with my family for a prolonged time. Thirteen days.

For weeks after that, Aster was certain the man was tailing her. Both Ivy and I took her seriously at first, never left her alone, but it turned out the guy had been sent to jail for racketeering shortly after the break-up.

That was around the time Aster was first diagnosed with schizophrenia.

One of the symptoms is paranoia.

"Well, it can't hurt to see who's inside the car," I mumble.

But no one's inside the car.

A cross dangles from the rearview mirror and a *Baby on Board* sticker decorates the bumper. Even though the glass is tinted, I make out two car seats and various toys. This does not strike me as the car of a vengeful gun-owner.

As I think this, a woman in heels teeters toward us, holding one infant in her arms and dragging another by the hand. She has a dinosaur sticker stuck to the hem of her dress.

"Can I help you?" Her tone tells me she's not looking to help us; she's looking to find out what we want with her car.

"Sorry, ma'am. My cousin has the same car. I thought he'd come to pick us up." I hate how easily lies are coming to me.

She shrugs. "Happens. Jeeps are popular." One of her kids screeches. "Since you're standing right there, mind getting the door?"

She beeps the car open, and I draw the door wide. She all but tosses the infant into the car seat, loops all these different straps around his flailing arms and legs, then kicks the door closed with her heel and goes around the car to get her other kid settled.

"Is it five o'clock yet?" she asks.

"No, ma'am, it's three-thirty."

"Must be five o'clock somewhere," she rambles, getting inside her car. And then she's pulling out of her spot so quick, Ivy and I have to jump out of the way.

"What happens at five?" I ask Ivy.

"Beats me."

As the Jeep exits the parking lot, I think of the man who almost choked on his meat. "Has Aster been taking her pills?" I ask.

"I don't think so. You know she hates it when I check."

"Can you check?"

"I'm going to have to." A rush of air escapes her lungs. "I hate playing bad cop all the time."

I touch Ivy's shoulder.

"Why can't I have normal worries? Like what I'm going to wear to school tomorrow, and who has the hots for whom?"

"'Cause you're exceptional. Not normal."

"That was *super* cheesy." She rolls her eyes.

"Cheesy's my middle name."

"I thought it was Hamster."

"Shut up."

"No, you shut up," she says, laughing.

I crack a grin. "I never thought it would make me laugh someday." But then I look back at Aster, and my glee wilts.

How am I going to tell her no one's following her? That it's all in her head? I ask Ivy this before returning to Aster.

"We're not going to tell her anything," she answers.

"I don't want to lie to her."

"And I don't want to hurt her. Sometimes, going along with someone's imaginings is kinder than challenging them."

Sadly, she's right.

"We need to get her back on her pills," Ivy adds with a sigh. "She'll be all right then."

On my way back to Aster, I text Jackie that I'm going to have to meet her some other time. I don't give her a reason because the reason scares the hell out of me.

I stash my phone back into my jeans. Aster's become chalk-white. I squeeze her hand, search her blue eyes.

I want to tell her she can stop making things up.

I want to tell her I'll keep her secret.

I want to tell her I understand why she did it.

I want to tell her I'm not mad at her for lying to me, for making me believe the Aster who bought the gun was someone other than her.

SEVENTEEN

While Ivy browses through the shelves of Goodwill, I stand by the shop window, peering out onto the parking lot.

"What do you think of these?" she asks me.

I glance at the pair of sandals clutched in her hands.

"They're nice," I say distractedly. At least I think they're nice. Why is she asking me? I'm not good with this sort of thing.

I go back to watching for the green Jeep. I can feel it's there, somewhere. Ivy and Josh saw a woman with two kids getting into the one in front of school, but I bet that was a ploy to lead me astray...to make me feel safe when I'm not.

"I'm ready to go. You want anything?" Ivy asks.

I finally turn away from the window and meet her at the cash register.

"That'll be twelve dollars," the salesperson says.

I start peeling money out of my Velcro wallet when Ivy's voice stops me.

"What are you doing?" she asks.

"Paying."

"I can see that, but why?"

"Isn't that—" I was going to say, *why I'm here*, but it might hurt my sister's feelings, so I rephrase it. "As a back-to-school present?" I fish out twelve singles.

"Aster," she says, pushing my hand away, "I got this."

"How?"

"I sewed some curtains for Miss Norbert over the weekend. She paid me two hundred dollars."

I blink. "You made two hundred dollars?"

"Yep." Ivy smiles proudly.

I'm too shocked to smile.

When we walk out of the shop, Ivy hands me the shopping bag. "They're for you." She tips her head to my feet.

Again, I blink. "You bought shoes for me?"

"One day, when I get famous, I'll buy you super nice ones...like, from Coach."

Her generosity stuns me into silence. I take the shoes out of the bag and really study them this time, run my fingers over each gold grommet and each black strap. Slowly, I crouch and take off the ones I'm wearing.

My feet are streaked with red indentations and blisters. Ivy winces at the sight, while I breathe a sigh of relief. I put the new ones on, tugging up the back zippers, waiting for them to pinch or press on some tender bone in my foot, but they don't. Instead of digging into my flesh, the leather straps are smooth and supple.

"I don't know what to say, Ivy."

"Just say you like them. You do, right?"

As I stand back up, my eyes brim with tears that end up spilling over.

Ivy pulls me into a hug. "I didn't mean to make you cry."

I sniffle. "Thank you."

"You're welcome, sis. Now let's go home. I promised Mom I'd help her hem her new quilt."

During the entire walk back home, I stare at my shoes.

While she tells me Sean asked her out on another date, I stare at my shoes.

While Ivy recommends I take medication I don't need, I stare at my shoes.

While I take said medication, I stare at my shoes.

Afraid they will vanish if I take them off, I keep them on to sleep.

KEEPING my car key wedged between my index and middle finger, I walk into Dr. Frank's office building. Ever since the Jeep started tailing me, I'm careful. Jackie once told me you could do serious damage with a key, so that's my weapon of choice.

The afternoon light is muted from the thick cover of clouds hanging over Kokomo. I wish it would rain already. I hate the stillness, the mugginess, the wait. The imminent storm reminds me of the stalking Jeep.

I ring the doctor's doorbell—because a little plaque on the door says *ring before entering*—then draw open the unlocked door. I'm early, so I sit on the brown corduroy couch by the window and scan the row of parked cars below. There's no Jeep, yet I feel as though I'm being watched.

I don't put my car key away. Instead, I inspect its sloping, jagged edges, and it makes me think of the key hanging around Mom's neck.

I slide my phone out of my backpack, open up a search page, and type: *Easy way to copy a key at home.*

I find a tutorial video that uses a lighter, clear packing tape, scissors, and a box of Tic Tacs. I watch it three times. By the third, I have it memorized. I put my phone away just as Dr. Frank's office door opens.

She ushers a young boy with severe acne and greasy black hair through the waiting room. I wonder what's wrong with him. Perhaps nothing. Perhaps he's like me and a concerned parent or sibling believes he needs someone to talk to.

"Aster, you can go inside. I'll be right there." Dr. Frank smiles that mouthful of ochre teeth that always makes me cringe.

She's pretty nice otherwise, but her teeth...

I put my phone and car key away in my backpack, then sling my bag over my shoulder. As I walk toward the gaping door, I pass the girl with the hairy legs. She stares unblinkingly back at me.

Sometimes, I want to ask her what's wrong, because— unlike me and the boy who just left—there's definitely something wrong with her. It's written all over her face.

I lower myself into the crackled, leather La-Z-Boy across from the flowery armchair Dr. Frank always sits in. Once she made us switch seats, and it really threw me. I wonder if she's made the boy switch seats yet. And then I wonder what chair the girl in the waiting room favors.

Dr. Frank returns, short, gray ponytail swooshing around the back of her head like a feather duster.

"What's wrong with her?" I ask.

"*Her?*" Dr. Frank takes a seat, pulls her yellow notebook out.

"The girl with the hairy legs in your waiting room. Why doesn't she shave her legs? Is it a fashion statement or is she afraid of sharp blades?"

"Oh...*her.*" Dr. Frank nods. "Perhaps she wants to be different? What do you think?"

I arch a brow. *Diagnosing is your job, not mine.* "I think she might be afraid of sharp blades."

"Are you afraid of sharp blades?"

"Me? No."

"Have you ever used any to harm yourself?"

I tried cutting myself once. To let out the darkness Mom filled me with. But nothing came out except blood. I don't tell Dr. Frank because I would never do it again, so there's no point in worrying her about it. I simply shake my head.

"How have you been feeling lately, Aster?" she asks.

I show her the new shoes Ivy bought me. Tell her that Josh kissed me. I don't tell her about the gun *or* the Jeep.

"These are wonderful occurrences." Dr. Frank flashes me that yellow smile of hers.

I try not to wince. It's rude to make people feel self-conscious. If my mother were the one sitting across from the doctor, she would already have made a comment. I pride myself on being nothing like Mom.

Dr. Frank dips her head toward the wall mirror behind me. Each session, she makes me stand up in front of it and tell my reflection five things I like about myself, external or internal. I usually get stuck at two. But she doesn't like it when I stop, so I always make three things up.

I stand up, letting my backpack tumble to my feet, and walk over to the wall. "My eyes. My beauty mark." I always say those two because I really do like my eyes, and Josh likes my beauty mark, so it must be nice. "I like the way my sandals fit on my feet." I stare at my reflection, at my blonde corkscrew curls that puff up around my cheekbones. I've already mentioned them in sessions, even though I'm not crazy about them. I bite my lip, observe my straight, white teeth. So unlike Mom's crooked ones. Thinking about my mother reminds me of the video tutorial I watched back in the waiting room. "My industriousness. And I like that I'm proactive."

Five. There. Done.

I return to my seat, fold one leg underneath me, and sit. "Those last two are new."

"The sandals too."

"The sandals too," she concedes, "but let's talk about those last two. How have you been industrious and proactive?"

Since I don't care to divulge my plan, I tell her I've been collecting recipes and testing them out regularly, and the results have been delicious.

Dr. Frank takes notes. At some point, she stands up, walks to her hang window, pulls it up, and lights a cigarette. She blows a cone of smoke through the side of her mouth.

The glowing embers remind me of the lighter I'll need to buy at CVS, along with Tic Tacs, sharp scissors, and clear packing tape. During the rest of my session, these four items scroll through my mind on a loop.

EIGHTEEN

JOSH

A dark green Jeep idles outside my gym.

Right next to my Camry.

Heart blasting, I stare around me, but the street is deserted. I walk around the Jeep. Take in the bumper sticker, the car seats, the messy backseat. What are the odds that the mother with the dinosaur sticker glued to her clothes is a member of my gym?

I jog back inside the gym. Few people are working out right now, and she's not one of them. Maybe she's in the locker room?

I burst into the women's changing room. One woman is unclipping her bra but stops when she spots me in the doorway. She stares at me, horrified. I take in the corridor-like space, listen for the sound of a shower or of a toilet flushing. It's quiet.

"Is anyone else in here?" I ask the flushed lady.

She snatches a towel from the bench to cover herself and shakes her head.

I mumble a quick apology, then head back out, scanning the room again. The woman I met in front of the twins' school isn't here. When I walk back out of the gym, I almost punch the hood of my car.

The Jeep's gone! It's freaking gone. *Poof.* Gone! I grab onto the roots of my hair, yank hard. How could I be so dumb? I should've waited. Stupid. That's what I am. *Stupid.*

The nape of my neck prickles as though I am being watched. My gaze zooms over the darkening street. Sure enough, I spot the Jeep's receding taillights. I leap into my car and crush the gas pedal, reversing out of my spot way too quickly.

Tires squealing, I take off in the direction of the Jeep. I turn the corner at full throttle. The car almost tips over, I'm pushing it so hard. I don't even care if I get fined for speeding. Jackie won't let a ticket stick once I explain my reason for burning rubber.

The Jeep turns left at the next intersection.

The left lane is clogged with cars, so I careen up my lane, then spin my wheel to the left just as the turn arrow becomes yellow. The car I cut off honks at me. Whatever. I made the light.

I've almost caught up with the Jeep, but it's weaving in and out of lanes. The woman knows I'm on her tail. She makes a sharp right, wheels biting into a curb. That's sure to destroy her rims.

I go after her.

The road ahead is a dead-end. I have her cornered.

But suddenly, the crazy woman starts backing up, at full throttle no less. Before she can convert my car into an accordion, I drive into the nearest yard, crushing an abandoned tricycle. The Jeep rockets back onto the main road, then lurches out of sight.

"Fuck!" I punch my steering wheel with an open hand. I owe my mother's curse jar another quarter.

I wrench my seatbelt off my chest and get out of the Camry to pull the squashed trike out from under my suspension. I don't want to roll over it a second time. Deep down, I'm also sort of hoping it's not totally broken, but the handle is bent parallel to the seat.

I let out a sigh that sounds an awful lot like a growl. I get back into the car and pull off the grass before returning to assess the rest of the damage—the lawn is ripped and bruised and will need to be reseeded, and there's a dent in the hedge lining the owner's walkway.

Still fuming, I walk to the front door and ring the doorbell. I hope the people will be reasonable and accept my offer to fix their yard myself. If they press charges, it'll cost me way more than the stupid chase was worth.

I still can't believe she got away!

It's a young girl who answers, a toddler sitting on her hip like a koala. I explain my little mishap. She explains she's the babysitter, that the parents aren't home yet. I leave my phone number with her.

I am an orb of nervous energy, overheated like the bare lightbulb that popped in our garage yesterday. The worst part though, is that I'm starting to doubt my cop potential. I should've been able to handle that car. Instead, I got out of its fucking way—*ping*.

I stop walking.

I still have the gun—*this* is what she's after.

She'll be back for it.

And this time, I'll be ready.

NINETEEN

After

The sky turned a burnt orange tonight, tinting the gray pavement the color of desert dunes and the hedges the color of molten chocolate. I wonder if Ivy saw it. She loves sunsets.

When I walk into the house, I find Mom in front of the TV, fingers laying listlessly on her lap, eyes wide open, zombie-like. My first thought is that she's dead. I check for a bullet wound, but remember Josh has the gun. Then again, if she procured herself *one* gun, she could probably buy another.

She doesn't turn toward me, and her chest isn't rising.

Maybe she overdosed.

I get this sick feeling inside my stomach, like I've swallowed a bag of nails and the pointy tips are embedding themselves inside the fleshy lining. I've always wished my mother would go away, but I never wished for her to die. I—

"What?" she huffs.

My heart kicks around in my chest.

She's not dead.

I should be relieved but I'm not. I'm—

"Why are you looking at me like that?"

I shut my gaping mouth, then slowly open it again to form words...a sentence. "I'm just surprised you're not working."

"I deserve a break sometimes."

I painted my toes bubblegum pink. I thought I used Ivy's nail polish, but she told me all her nail polishes are on top of our dresser, not in the bathroom where I found the pink one. I was going to rub it off before Mom noticed I borrowed something of hers, but there was no nail polish remover.

I squeeze the CVS bag in my hand. Pink acetone sloshes in its plastic bottle, clinking against the Tic Tac box, the scissors, the lighter, the roll of packing tape.

I should've used the nail polish remover before entering the apartment, but I assumed Mom would be in her studio, working, not on the couch, vegetating.

The ceiling light isn't on, so I doubt she can see my painted toenails. Still, I step toward the couch and tuck my feet underneath its base.

"Do you know where Ivy is?" she asks me.

"I thought she'd be here."

Mom frowns. "Well, she isn't."

I try moving but my bones feel like they've fused together. "Want something to eat? I was about to make dinner..."

Mom tilts her head down. "Sure, but don't make anything too fancy. I know Maggie loves her complicated, unpronounceable French dishes, but you should be able to pronounce what you eat."

I walk briskly to the fridge and pull it open to see what's inside. Grated cheddar. Half a carton of cream. Half a head of lettuce. Orange juice. "Penne with cream sauce?"

"Okay." Making sure Mom's attention is on the lit screen again, I edge back out of the kitchen and walk down the narrow corridor to the bathroom. As soon as I'm inside, I ball some cotton, soak it in the remover, and strip my nails of their pretty pinkness. I place the bottle on one of the shelves and am about to close the mirrored door when I spy a bottle of sleeping pills. I shake out a few, then screw the lid back on and replace the bottle. I toss the used cotton in the toilet and flush it down, then stop by my room to stow the rest of my purchases inside my underwear drawer.

Pills stuffed snugly inside my jeans' pocket, I return to the kitchen to make dinner.

***

"YOU LIKE IT?" I tip my chin toward Mom's almost-empty bowl.

The tines of her fork scour the thick ceramic, scraping up the last lumps of congealed sauce. "You put in too much cheese, but I was hungry."

I want to ask why she can't simply say *yes it was good*, or *thank you for making dinner, Aster*. How hard is it to say something nice? Does she think it will make her appear weak or soft? Or does she think it will weaken *me*? She's wrong. Kindness makes people stronger; it makes people believe in themselves; it makes them feel necessary and important— and I don't mean conceited, I mean useful.

"I wanted to speak to you about the gun," she says suddenly.

My spine tautens. Is she going to accuse me again? Ask why I did it? Will she listen when I tell her…again…that even though my name was on the registration, it wasn't mine?

She shuts her eyes, rubs her forehead, massages her temples. "*I bought it.*"

I gape at her. This feels like an apology. Mom never apologizes.

Her lids come up. She looks at me, then beyond me at the door. "If you tell Ivy, I'll deny it."

I've managed to wedge my mouth closed even though the aftershock of her words lingers. "Why?"

"Because I felt unsafe. We live on the ground floor. We're only women—"

"I didn't mean, why did you buy it? I meant, why did you pin it on me?"

She takes a deep breath, wipes the back of her hand across her eyes. "I thought I was losing Ivy to you."

I don't tell her, *it's not a competition, Mom,* because I'm acutely aware that it is…it always has been. Mom and I have constantly jousted for Ivy's affection and attention, because winning them gives us purpose and importance.

I toy with a loose thread on the hem of my T-shirt. "How did you get them to put my name on the registration?"

She sucks on her bottom lip and glances over at the TV. "I asked a friend to buy the gun."

"And her name happened to be Aster like me?"

"Funny, huh?"

She's lying. I feel it in my bones. She must've found my fake ID and used it.

She yawns. "Why do I feel so tired?"

My cheeks flush with color that I pray she doesn't spot.

Over the next five minutes, her lids lower as though tiny weights were attached to her translucent lashes. I think about the sleeping pills I ground into her sauce and the handful of cheese I added at the last minute, worried she would detect the chalky flavor or powdery texture.

When she falls asleep, I don't feel an ounce of regret for what I have done or for what I'm about to do.

I carry our empty bowls of pasta into the kitchen, pour scalding water over Mom's to erase all traces of the pills. The sound of the tap running doesn't bother her sleep. What if she never awakens? What if I put too many pills?

No. She'll be fine, I reason. I only used three. Four at the most.

After I set the bowls to dry on the rack, I go collect my supplies from my bedroom. With shaky fingers, I empty the orange Tic Tacs right into my drawer, then cut out one of the sides of the box. I bring my makeshift tools into the living room and lay them out on the coffee table like a surgeon about to operate.

Drool leaks out of Mom's mouth. I scoot closer to her.

My breathing stills, but not my heart.

The key is tucked inside her blouse. I hoist the string up. When the glare of the TV screen glints off the metal, I suck in my breath. I carefully liberate it from the blouse. I cut a piece of clear packing tape, but because my fingers shake, it folds on itself. I crumple it and cut off another piece, this time more carefully.

I stick it to the edge of the coffee table, then cut out two more strips—backups—and tape them to the table also. Next, I grab the lighter. Praying the scent of fire won't wake Mom, I hold the key away from her flammable shirt and warm the metal. It heats up so quickly, it singes my index finger and thumb. I almost drop the key, but if I drop it now, it'll wake Mom, so I endure the burn. Once the metal has blackened, I toss the lighter on the cushion next to me and wait for the key to cool down.

Sweat drips down the sides of my face, beads on my nose. I don't wipe it away. After enough time has passed, I seize one of the pieces of tape and press the sticky side against the metal.

Like in the tutorial, a blackened imprint appears on the clear tape. I set the key down against Mom's rising chest, then carefully glue the tape on the section of Tic Tac box. Latching on to the scissors, I reverentially swipe the square of plastic from the table and return to my bedroom. I don't have a lock on my door, so I keep my back against it as I cut out each crenellated edge.

More perspiration forms on my face, drips into my mouth, salty and wet like tears. I barely breathe as I incise the plastic. Closing one eye, I hold my creation up to the ceiling light to inspect my handiwork. I snip off a tiny piece of excess clear plastic, then inspect my intricate design again. This time the plastic shape matches up to the black imprint perfectly. How I managed this with shaky fingers is an absolute miracle.

My heart leaps against the ramparts of my chest. Mom will never be able to hide anything from me again. Not a gun, not anything.

I set the scissors aside on the bookshelf, on top of a pile of dog-eared Western romance paperbacks I recovered from a trash bin, and open my bedroom door, wincing when it creaks.

I ball my fingers, making a protective fist around my plastic key. The grooves and indents bite into my skin. Heart pumping madly, I creep back into the living room. Mom's eyes are still shut, her chest still rising evenly, the key still resting on her cheap blouse.

I tread quietly to her studio and am about to let myself in when Mom makes a loud snorting sound.

I drop my hands back to my sides, lurch away from the door like a ballerina. Panic rises, tangy like vomit, in my throat. Mom stirs, moves her head from side to side. I wait for her lids to spring upward; I wait for her pallid gaze to set on me; for her thin mouth to pinch.

My fists feel like rocks against my hips, hard in spite of their wobbliness. Mom's lids remain shut, and then she's immobile again.

For long seconds, all I do is breathe. Try to return some oxygen to my depleted lungs before they shrivel like the first strip of packing tape. When I feel calmer, I edge toward the studio again.

With clammy fingers that no longer feel attached to my palms, I turn the doorknob, and press the door open, then slide my quivering body inside and shut the door softly behind me. I don't spin the twist lock because it always makes a sharp grating noise, like a bullet.

I tiptoe across the room and kneel in front of the drawer. And then, whispering a little prayer, I fit the piece of plastic into the lock.

It slides right in.

TWENTY

JOSH

The sweat on my temples has turned icy by the time I pull out of the dead-end street. I lower my window to let the warm night air dry the frosty dampness. I'm also hoping it will ease my nerves. Thaw me out like a microwave defrosts frozen stuff.

My knuckles are bone-white. My fingers too. I relax my death grip on my steering wheel, but I don't unsquash my lips. I drive to Aster's. I need to tell her I trust her. That I never meant not to trust her.

No, I won't tell her that. It will only hurt her.

I try calling to tell her I'm coming over, but she doesn't answer her cell. So I dial her home number. It rings and rings.

Scenarios start spooling through my mind.

Wild scenarios.

The crazy lady in the green Jeep went to Aster's house.

Driving me off the road was a diversion. She's going to hold Aster hostage until I hand over the gun. She must be working with Rose. Maybe she's another patient of Rose's shrink, because who drives someone off the road? Who stalks teenagers?

I think about her kids. Pity them. Cracked people shouldn't be allowed to raise children.

Yet they do.

Everyday.

Everywhere.

I think of Aster and Ivy and all they've endured.

I call Aster's phone. Nothing. I call Ivy.

"She's at home, Josh. Why?"

I don't tell her why. I don't want to worry her.

"Just looking for her."

"Okay. Well I need to get back to studying. I'll see you later?"

"Yeah. Maybe."

I hang up, then phone the Redds' home phone again. Still no one picks up.

Heart thundering, I speed down the shadowy roads toward Mulberry Street.

TWENTY-ONE

Mom's standing in the doorway of her studio, one hand on the knob, the other on the doorframe. Even though no light is on, her eyes blaze in the obscurity.

Ivy always jokes the ringtone of our house phone is loud enough to wake the dead. I don't know about the dead, but it woke Mom.

I slam her special drawer shut and rip the plastic key out of the lock, and then I stand to face the retaliation that's sure to be vicious.

My gaze darts to the big pair of scissors tucked into a shelf on her sewing table. I don't take them, but make sure they're within reach.

Mom sways into the room, woozy with sleep.

I feel like I have a sharp blade inside my chest instead of

a heart. Mom's hand comes up and arcs through the air toward my cheek. When it comes down, my face flies sideways. My skin smarts and prickles and burns.

I don't cry.

"How dare you, Aster? How dare you!" She grabs my wrist, forces my fingers open, then rips the serrated piece of plastic out of my fingers.

In the moonlight, she studies it. And then she hits me again.

This time, I fold like a chopped tree trunk. My knees and palms hit the ground first. And then my head knocks into the hard and cold five-star base of Ivy's chair. The world turns ghost-white, then chrome-yellow, before crackling back to its hushed blueness.

"I've always respected your privacy. Always. I never pried. Never went inside your bedroom. Never looked through your stuff. But if that's how you want to play it, then that's how we'll play it."

She takes off toward the living room, spidery legs no longer affected by the drugs. I scramble to my feet and run after her. She makes it to my room before I do. She pulls open the dresser's top drawer, yanks out handfuls of clothes, and throws them around. Orange Tic Tacs flutter out like confetti. She closes her fingers around the little porcelain box containing my milk teeth. I grab onto her arm before she can lob it at the floor.

"Mom, stop! I didn't see anything! I didn't see anything!"

She doesn't stop. Wrenches her arm out of my grasp and throws my keepsake box. It soars through the air and lands on a pile of dirty clothes I planned to wash later.

Mom yanks open the next drawer. Ivy's candy-colored clothes spray around us like the cool water from the sprinklers we used to run through on sticky summer days. Rooted to the ground, I watch as Mom sweeps her arm across the dresser top, sending all of Ivy's nail polishes crashing to the floor. A framed baby picture of Ivy and me sails down next. The glass fractures, falls in big shards around the silver frame.

When Mom edges toward my bookcase, I stand before it, like a warrior guarding her soldiers. I extend my arms. Yell for her to stop. She advances toward me, fury burning in her narrowed eyes.

"Mrs. Redd!"

I fling my attention to the doorway.

Josh is here.

I blink to make sure my mind isn't playing tricks on me.

He's really here.

Josh has come to help me.

"How—" I croak. I want to ask how he knew I needed him, but the words die when Mom's hands jerk me aside. I collide into the wall like a ragdoll. Josh lunges toward me, catches me while Mom wreaks havoc, tossing my books, ripping pages, shredding them.

Though my head is swimming, though my eyes burn, though Josh is trying to shelter me behind his broad body, I keep my eyes on my ravaged possessions.

Mom's eyes meet mine over Josh's shoulder. They gleam with surprise? Fear? Understanding? "You are not worthy of his name," she says, voice as thick and tense as the air pulsating between our three bodies.

Without looking away from my face, she picks up the fallen scissors, shreds my plastic key into tiny, clear slivers, and flings the shards at me, but they hit Josh's chest instead.

Flit down to his feet.

"Let's go," he says roughly.

Rivers of tears course over my cheeks, drip off my chin.

I stop putting up resistance and let Josh guide me out of my devastated room.

"You betrayed me, Aster," Mom bellows, following us into the living room.

I wince. I want to answer, "You betrayed me first," but my lips tremble too much to form words. I keep my eyes on my shuffling feet, on the flashing grommets of my sandals, as I walk.

"How?" I ask him once I'm sitting in his car. "How did you know to come?"

Green eyes fixed on the road, he says, "I just felt it."

I smile. In spite of the horror of tonight, in spite of my tumbling tears, I smile.

Josh felt me.

He felt *me*.

TWENTY-TWO

JOSH

After Aster falls asleep in the guest bedroom, I head downstairs to where Mom and Jackie are having a glass of wine.

When I thundered into the house, cradling Aster against me, when they took in her bloated, tear-streaked face, the green bulge on her forehead, they fell terribly quiet. They didn't try to intercept her and sit her down for questioning.

They knew.

They just knew.

The years have connected us in wordless ways.

"She needs to be placed in an institution. She's a danger to her children and a danger to herself," I tell them, grinding my fingers into fists. "Aster can't go back there."

Mom's placed her hand over my shoulder. She's trying to soothe me, but her effort is wasted. I am beyond manic tonight. Like a pressure cooker, I've reached my boiling point. Anger spews from every pore on my body.

"Six months, Josh. Six months," Mom's saying.

"Did you not see the bruise on Aster's forehead?" I'm shaking. "That woman is crazy! She needs to be interred."

"Interned," Jackie says quietly. "I'm pretty sure we'd get arrested if we buried Rose."

I stare at her. "What are you talking about?"

A laugh erupts from Mom. She claps her palm against her mouth, but it only mutes the bubbling sound. "I'm sorry. Nerves." And then she's crying laughing.

And I still don't get what's going on.

Jackie bites her lip. "Josh, does Aster want to press charges?"

"I didn't ask her." After a beat where the only sound is my mother's dying laughter, I ask, "Can she?"

"Does Rose have a gun?" Jackie asks.

"What?" I go still. "How—" My words die out when she flicks her gaze to Mom. "How do *you* know, Mom?"

She wipes her eyes, smudging some of her mascara. "The phone call in front of the bakery. You asked Ivy if Rose had a gun, and then a couple nights later, Aster's at our house and I guessed something was going on. So I called Ivy and she told me about Mr. Mancini's cat."

"You knew all along?"

Mom's sober again. She nods.

"And you?" I ask the cop in street clothes nursing a glass of wine.

She takes a deep breath, pushes her glass of wine away, leans her forearms against the white marble kitchen island. "I guessed something was going on when you dropped by the precinct, but I didn't know it had to do with a gun until right now."

"Ivy says the gun's registered to her sister," Mom adds.

"Yeah," I answer, "but Aster didn't buy it."

"Are we sure of that?" Mom asks.

"'Cause if she did, Josh," Jackie putts in, "then she must've forged an ID to fake her age, and, well, that's not going to help once we get the twins in front of a judge."

"She didn't buy it!" I repeat, hating that they don't trust Aster.

"How can you be sure?" Jackie asks.

"Because I am." Maybe they'd stop asking questions if I told them that a car drove me off the road tonight, that it's been tailing Aster ever since we stopped by the firearms shop. But what's the point in panicking Mom? Besides, I don't want to get the police involved.

I started this mess when I ran the trace; I will finish this mess. Even if it means running down my street, waving a gun in my hand. If the crazy Jeep lady knows where Aster lives, she knows where I live too.

"Does Rose still have the gun?" Jackie asks.

"No."

"Where is it?"

"I gave it back to the shop."

"Why'd you do that?" Jackie says, springing away from the countertop. "You should've given it to me, Josh. It's evidence."

"Evidence? There was no murder..." I say. Besides Mancini's cat. *Poor creature.*

"But if Rose used it to threaten her daughters—"

I interrupt Jackie. "It'll be her word against theirs."

Suddenly, the door bursts open. I expect to see my dad but it's Ivy. She careens into the kitchen, skin pasty and mouth gaping open. "What the hell happened at my house?

Where's Aster?" Her voice is so harsh I'm afraid it'll wake up her twin. "Why'd she trash our room?"

"*She* didn't. It was your mom."

She jolts back, blinks. "But Mom said…"

"That it was Aster?" I finish for her. Shake my head. "Your mom blames your sister for everything that's wrong in her life."

"But—" Ivy gapes at Jackie and Mom. "Why would she do that?"

"Aster wouldn't tell me what happened." I tried to get her to talk but she was too stressed out to utter a single word. "I'm surprised your mom didn't tell you."

"She said Aster flipped out."

"I was there, Ivy. It was your mom who *flipped out.*"

My friend mulls this over, then asks, "Where is Aster?"

"Upstairs. Sleeping."

Ivy fords across the kitchen. I'm about to stop her but think Aster will be glad to see her sister.

"She's not going back there. I won't let her."

Ivy freezes.

"And you shouldn't go back there either. You're not safe."

"What are we supposed to do? Get tossed into the foster care system for six months?"

"You can move in with us," Mom says. It's not the first time she's offered them refuge.

"We can't, Maggie. You've been more than kind over the years, have done more than anyone has ever done for us, but we can't just abandon our mother. She's not well. She wouldn't survive without us."

"Aster won't survive *with* her," I say.

"I never forced Aster to come home with me. Never."

"Yet she comes back each time *for* you."

"But I don't ask her to."

I snort. "She cares about you more than she cares about anyone!"

"Calm down, Josh," Mom says.

I toss my hands in the air. "How am I supposed to calm down?"

Mom, Jackie, and Ivy exchange a look. And then Ivy turns the corner and heads up the stairs. Her light footsteps resonate against our carpeted pine floors and then fade once she enters the guestroom.

"I'll stop by their apartment on my way home," Jackie says in a low voice, tugging her coat from the hook by our front door.

"Will you arrest her?" I ask.

She lowers her gaze to the umbrella stand, thanks Mom for the wine, then leaves without answering me.

"Have you had dinner yet, honey?" Mom asks after Jackie leaves.

I shake my head.

"Do you want me to make you a plate?"

I drag my hands down the sides of my face. "Yes. No. I don't know."

Shoulders pinched, she opens the oven door, scoops roasted meat and carrots onto a plate, then places it in front of me. "You mind if I wait for your dad? He doesn't like eating alone."

I shake my head, shovel down the food that tastes hot.

Ivy comes down a few moments after I finish eating. She hasn't regained much color. If anything, she seems more gray than white. "She won't tell me what happened," she says softly, then sighs as she takes a seat next to me. She places her hand on top of mine, squeezes it. "Thank you for bringing her here. I don't know what we would do without you in our lives." She bumps her shoulder into mine.

And for the first time since I left the gym, I breathe a little easier.

"It might be the new meds," Ivy says. "That made Mom act"—she swallows—"the way she did."

I don't believe it has anything to do with her medication.

"She said something strange tonight," I suddenly say.

"Who?"

"Your mom."

"Mom? Say something strange?"

It's a paltry attempt at a joke, but I smile a little. "She told Aster: *you are not worthy of his name.* What does that mean?"

"God's name?" Mom suggests, dipping her lips into her glass of wine.

"Rose isn't religious."

"It's weird, but not the weirdest thing she's ever said. Recently she told me I was going to marry a man who'll live among horses and chickens."

"What?" I ask.

"Yeah. Apparently, her psychic told her I'm going to get hitched to a farmer." She grins widely, and it gives her cheeks some pinkness. "Me. The girl who dreams of living in a big city. Who dreams of fame and fortune."

I chuckle. "You'll just be fortunate if you can find a man who can deal with your passion for sewing."

"Hey!" Ivy flicks me.

I laugh now.

A wide grin splitting her face, Ivy continues telling stories we already know. Stories of the strange things her mother has done and said over the years. And it humanizes that hateful woman, but it doesn't spark any forgiveness in me.

Broken people shouldn't try to break others.

TWENTY-THREE

Asher

J osh's scent is everywhere. I pull in a lungful of air from my dark bedroom. I swear I can smell him, and yet, when was the last time he laid in my bed?

My bed.

My bedroom.

Mom.

My lids slam up in time with my upper body. Sitting, I blink to make out my surroundings. I'm not in my bed, not in my house. I find Josh lying on his stomach, head on the pillow next to mine, wearing gray boxers and a Metallica T-shirt.

Heat snakes through me. Like a belly-dancer, it writhes and fills each corner of my soul with warmth and love.

Gently, so as not to wake him, I lie back down and snuggle against him.

Visions of the evening file through my mind. They feel surreal. Half dream, half nightmare. Even though my audacity was punished brutally, squashed and shattered, it thrills me. I've never felt so strong and cunning, able to accomplish anything. Yes, I have no more key, but deep down, I know that if I ever have doubts about what Mom hides inside her drawer, I can make a new one.

I've done it once. I can do it again.

Besides, tonight, I learned one other thing.

A thing of vital importance to me.

Ivy didn't lie to me. Inside Mom's drawer, there really were only rolls of fabric. Glittery, soft, crinkly, beaded. I'm not sure why she locks them up, but then again, I'm not sure why my mother does most things.

Well, besides to drive a wedge between Ivy and me.

She failed.

She will always fail at that.

Nothing could ever separate Ivy and me.

You can't chop one person in two and hope one half stays alive and not the other. Human bodies don't work like that. Ivy and me, we're one. She cannot make us two.

Audacious and victorious.

I trail my fingers over Josh's bent arm, over the fine hairs bleached by the sun, over the soft skin burnished by the long hot summer. I touch the smooth, tanned planes of his face next. And then I get bolder and press my lips against his.

His mouth softens against mine. His lips move against mine. Soon, his breathing intensifies, and his hands skate over my skin. He shifts onto his side, opens his eyes.

"Hey."

"Hey," I whisper through tipped-up lips.

He touches my forehead lightly, and it smarts. The memory of the base of Ivy's chair flashes through my mind then back out.

Thank you, I mouth. *And not simply for tonight but for the last four thousand three hundred and eighty days of our lives.*

I don't say this out loud, but I think it as I press him onto his back and straddle him.

The butterflies have returned in numbers tonight, and they are performing backflips inside my belly. Tonight, I am made entirely of butterflies. There are no more contemplations and emotions inside of me, no more considerations and decisions.

Only instinct and need.

Only the man I've landed on.

Or rather the one who landed on me twelve years ago.

TWENTY-FOUR

JOSH

Aster and I have decided to tell Ivy about us. She'll do the telling while I drive the gun over to the precinct. I plan on handing it over to Jackie and letting her investigate its provenance. Hopefully it will lead to the arrest of psycho Jeep-lady.

As I take the street that leads to the precinct, I catch a glimpse of dark green in my rearview mirror.

"Unbelievable," I whisper. The woman just won't stop.

I ogle my phone. It would be a good time to call Jackie. She'd come out and arrest Jeep-lady right then and there.

Instead, I keep driving. When I turn right on South Lafountain, and the Jeep turns right, I know I've got it hooked to my bumper. Exhilaration throttles through me.

I know exactly how I'm going to trap Jeep-lady.

Even though I detailed my car three days ago, I hang a left in the middle of the block and pull into Mason's Drive-

Through Car Wash. The Jeep slows to a crawl further down and enters the Walgreen's parking lot. It's no longer in my field of vision, but I'm pretty sure it won't be going anywhere until *I* go somewhere.

The white Toyota in front of me enters the car wash. I go ahead and purchase a token from the drive-through attendant. From the looks of his pimply skin and sparse chin hairs, I assume he's sixteen, give or take a year. The guy eyes my car, frowns—he must notice the Camry doesn't need a wash—but takes my money anyway. Maybe he thinks I'm OCD or something.

I drive onto the automated rails, then jump out, hauling my gym bag.

"What are you doing?" the dude asks, wide-eyed.

I jerk my chin toward Walgreen's. "I'm working under-cover, and I need your help." I haven't put in my token yet. "Drive my car through the wash, then head into the Walgreen's lot and park it. I'll meet you there."

"You serious, man?"

"Yeah. I called for backup but they're fifteen minutes out." Surprise and doubt mash on the attendant's face.

"Can I see your badge?"

"No time for that. Here." I shove the keys in his hands. "This is a matter of national security."

He blinks.

I lay a reassuring palm on his scrawny arm. "You got this. Just stay in the car, all right?"

Finally, he moves. Straight for the open door of the Camry. After he gets in and shuts the door, I insert the token and then run around the large white building.

I edge around the side until I can see the back of the Walgreen lot.

I watch the Jeep.

Detect a presence inside.

I feel like Led Zeppelin's drummer is inside my chest, beating my heart like he used to pound his drums.

I text Jackie: **Rendezvous Walgreens on South Lafountain**. I toss the bag and the phone on the ground, and dig out the gun, sliding it into my jeans' waistband.

And then I wait some more.

My nostrils pulse with furious breaths.

I see the front hood of my car pop out of the car wash, and then, exactly like I asked, the attendant drives onto South Lafountain and takes a sharp left into the adjacent lot.

Knowing Jeep-lady's attention will be on my car, I race across the concrete field toward the back end of the lot like a running back and slide-lunge behind the first parked car. Ducking, I dash from one car to the next until I've arrived next to the Jeep.

With slick fingers, I grab the gun from my waistband, and slurping in an insane amount of air and courage, I jerk upright and point the gun at the passenger window.

The person at the wheel startles, but not as much as I do when I make out the face of my stalker through the tinted window.

TWENTY-FIVE

Aster

There are so many things I want to tell my sister. And in time, I'll tell her everything, but some will have to wait until we no longer live under Mom's roof.

Ivy picks a piece of crumble off the top of her raspberry muffin. We are sitting in Maggie's bakery that's overrun with pudgy-limbed toddlers and their legging-clad mothers. We should be in school, but we spent our morning picking up the debris inside our bedroom and salvaging our possessions after Mom locked herself in her studio.

Ivy told me Mom felt bad about what she'd done, that she'd panicked because she couldn't find her key and thought I'd taken it. But then she'd located it. It was wedged between the couch cushions.

I'm not sure why she lied. Perhaps she did it because she

felt guilty about the gun she pinned on me. Or perhaps she didn't mention my plastic key because she thought it undermined her authority.

"She told me she asked a friend to buy her the gun for protection," my twin says.

"She used my fake ID," I say.

"She said her friend was called—"

"You fell for that?"

Ivy gapes at me. Slowly, she wipes the astonishment off her face with a sigh. "I'm sorry, Asty. I wish she'd used mine."

When I made my ID, I made my sister a matching one. She doesn't use it to sneak into R-rated movies, though; she uses it to buy beer and get into clubs.

I raise a stiff smile. "I'm glad she didn't involve you."

Ivy smiles back, and it's like peering at a mirror, because her smile is as strained as mine, and her eyes are as puffy as mine, and her skin is as sallow as mine. Neither of us slept much last night.

Funny thing is though, last night was possibly the worst and best of my life.

"I need to tell you something," I say, nibbling on my nails that are already bitten to the quick.

"You're going to press charges?"

"What?" When I get that she means Mom, I look down. "I haven't decided yet."

I haven't decided because I feel like I owe Mom for her discretion. I never thought I would owe my mother for anything besides giving me life.

Ivy's forehead is creased. "I don't think she would survive losing us."

"Losing *you*," I correct.

Ivy doesn't correct me. She takes a bite of her muffin instead and chews slowly, pensively.

I feel Maggie watching us from behind the counter. I give her a quick smile to reassure her that everything's okay. Her brightly painted lips bend upward in response. When her attention drifts back to the customer pointing to the tray of red velvet cupcakes, I lean across the small round table so the next thing I tell my sister will reach her ears and hers alone. "There's something else I need to tell you."

Ivy's gaze detaches from the moist, flecked confection in her hands.

"Josh and I, we're...we're together."

The half-eaten muffin tumbles out of her fingers and onto the plate. After a beat, she blurts out, "Like a couple?"

I nod.

Her blue eyes widen and fix on my identical ones. She gapes at me so long without saying a word that I think she's mad.

My stomach flip-flops. "Are you angry?"

"Angry?" She straightens. "No. Just...surprised. How long has this been going on?"

"Almost two weeks."

"Two weeks!" she squeaks.

I nod.

She makes a face. "That's why he's been acting so bizarre lately. Coming to school with BLTs and—"

"I really love him, you know?" A blush creeps up my throat, splatters my jaw, paints my cheeks red.

For a moment, she doesn't say anything, and no emotion registers on her face. "I know. I do too. Not in that way, though. Don't worry." She catches my drumming fingers in hers and squeezes them hard. "I'm so happy for you guys. This is the best news I've had in a while."

I scrutinize her face to make sure she's not lying to reassure me. There is true joy in her gaze.

She leans over, whispers conspiratorially. "Have you told Maggie?"

"Not yet. We wanted to tell you first."

She grins. "I'm happy you did. It means a lot to me."

Just like her approval means everything to me.

"So...how did it happen?" she asks.

I'm about to tell her about the movies, when I spy an abandoned magazine on the table next to ours. It sits beside an empty porcelain mug marred by lipstick-stains. I reach over and pick up the magazine.

On the glossy page, staring wide-eyed back at me, hairy legs pulled into her chest, sits the girl from Dr. Frank's waiting room.

"Aster?" Ivy says, trying to catch my attention.

I point to her. "I know her. She goes to see Dr. Frank too."

Ivy's gaze roams over the page and a small groove appears between her eyebrows. "Are you sure?"

"How many girls with hairy legs do you know?"

"Not many, but this looks like an advertisement. Which probably means she's a model."

Being different is okay is written in a pretty yellow font over the girl's troubled face.

She sits the same way at Dr. Frank's waiting room. With her legs pulled up underneath her chin. "She must be a spokesperson."

My sister frowns. "Maybe. Anyway, tell me about your first date."

I flip the magazine over, replacing the girl's sad eyes with my sister's happy ones.

TWENTY-SIX

JOSH

I gape at the man in the driver's seat as he lowers the passenger window. Keeping my gun trained on him, I search the backseat for the crazy mother who ran me off the road. Only thing back there are the two car seats. "Where's the...where is she?"

"Can you put the gun away, Joshua?"

I swing my gaze back to him, squeeze the gun tighter, put my finger on the trigger. He knows my name.

"I'll explain, but not at gunpoint. You either lower the gun and get in, or I will back out of here, and you'll stay in the dark."

"I have a gun. You don't. You don't get to make the rules."

Out of nowhere, he points a pistol pimped out with a long cylindrical silencer at me. "Get in the car before your friend over there calls the cops."

"They're already on the way."

"Then I'll be on mine."

He reverses the car. I jolt backward. Before he can roll off, I lunge toward the passenger door. "Okay. Okay. Let me get my car keys."

"No time."

The distant wail of sirens pierces the quiet afternoon.

Shooting the drive-through attendant an apologetic look, I jump into the Jeep. Although the dude's face isn't completely unfamiliar, I can't place him. He's put his gun down, but I haven't. I glide one of my hands over my jeans' back pocket to grab my phone, but it's not there.

I left it in my gym bag!

Heart banging, I curse my stupidity, then wrap my hand back around the gun. "Do we know each other?" My voice rings in my ears.

"Put the gun away," he says, his voice a low rumble.

"Hell, no."

He spins the wheel of the Jeep so hard the velocity pins me to the door and unbalances my aim. He seizes the gun from my clammy fingers with such little effort I wonder if I was even holding on to it.

"Kids shouldn't play with guns."

"But psycho stalkers should?"

One side of his mouth hitches up. "Psycho stalker?"

"You've been following us with your sidekick. You even used children to lure us into thinking—"

"My wife isn't my sidekick, and my kids aren't bait."

"But—"

"I've been using her car while mine's in the shop."

It hits me why he's familiar. "You're that security guard! Aster Colson!"

"Private agent, not security guard."

Even his voice sounds familiar, but that's impossible. And yet—

I'm jerked around in my seat. Snapping out of my trance, I look around. We're in the middle of a deserted construction site. He slides the Jeep underneath the metal foundations of a building as huge as my old high school.

Cold sweat beads on my upper lip.

He's brought me here to kill me.

Instead of thinking up ways of escaping, I think of my mother, Aster, Ivy, and Dad, and hope they'll think I was kidnapped. If they know I willingly jumped into a car with a madman, they'll be so disappointed. On the upside, it might make my death easier on them.

I can already hear my eulogy: "He wasn't very bright, but he was kind."

I blink away my macabre thoughts. I'm not dying today. *Nope. Not ready.*

I run through what Jackie taught me about criminals. The best way to distract them is to keep them talking. Hostage negotiation was her specialty back in the day. "The owner of the gun shop called you and told you about me and Aster?"

He puts the car in park, then glances at me. His hand is on the Glock. He's stroking the barrel as though it were a woman's thigh.

He doesn't seem to be listening to me, so I continue, "Why did you chase us around instead of simply asking us for your gun back? You out of jobs or something?"

"You ask a lot of questions."

"You said you'd explain."

He stops stroking the gun, looks up. His eyes are startlingly blue in contrast to his light brown skin. He reminds me of that baseball player. What's his name again—

"I've been searching for this gun a long time," he says, interrupting my straying thoughts.

This is *so not* the time to think about who he reminds me of.

"I thought I'd lost it but..." His gaze lands on something beyond me.

I shift around in my seat, relief and fear warring inside my torso. Has someone come to help him, or help me?

There's no one there.

Anxiety crawls up my throat like a worm on Ritalin. "But what?"

"But now I know it was stolen from me. By a woman no less. Not that I have anything against women."

"You mean *Rose* stole your gun?"

"Rose," he repeats softly. "Can't believe she's the one who stole my gun...." A wan smile settles over his lips.

"How do you even know her?"

He tilts his head down, studies me with his intensely bright eyes. I blink because I think I'm seeing Ivy. She always makes that face when she's considering something. "We had a thing almost twenty years ago," he finally says. "I was on leave back then, so it didn't last long. Two weeks." He lowers his eyes to the gun, studies its lines and contours. "And I didn't ring your doorbell, Joshua, because I needed to understand what two kids were doing with my gun. Especially since one of them had my name. So when my buddy gave me Aster's address—Mulberry Street—I drove out there. And then you text me asking if I know a Rose Redd. And everything falls into place." His gaze locks onto mine. "I didn't mean to scare you kids, but I didn't want to leave my gun in some stranger's possession. I'd never declared it lost or stolen, so if it was ever used, it would've been one hell of a shitfest."

"Rose never mentioned you," I say.

"I don't think I was worth mentioning." Something akin to regret makes his eyes murky. "You see, I lied to her. Told her I sold fabric because that's what she liked. I even bought her all these colorful rolls of satin and beaded silks to make myself feel better about lying." He snorts, even though a small smile plays on his lips. "And how does the woman repay me? She steals my gun. She was cunning, that one." He rubs his hand over his closely-cropped hair. "Have I answered all your questions, Joshua?"

A realization squirms into my brain. Rose said, *You don't deserve his name.* Could *his* refer to the man sitting across from me? As though I'd been sleeping and someone poured a bucket of iced water over me, I wake up.

Like, really wake up.

"You're their father," I whisper-yell-gasp.

"What?" He shakes his head. "No."

"Yes!" This is why he looked familiar! Not because of his website photo, not because he resembled a baseball player, but because of the color of his eyes, the angles of his jawline, the shape of his mouth, the shade of his skin.

"Those twins aren't mine."

"One of them even has *your* name!"

His pupils throb. "Rose would've told me—"

"Not if she was scared of you."

"Scared of me?"

"What sort of fabric salesman carries a gun?" I say way too loudly, but it's hard to contain my excitement. "When Rose found your gun, she must've freaked, and when she got pregnant, well, she probably thought she was protecting her daughters by not involving you." The tension that's been oozing inside me for the past few weeks finally diffuses. "There's no doubt in my mind that you're their father!" I declare, feeling more winded than when I lift for two hours straight.

This time, he doesn't contradict me. He merely sits there, mute and dumbfounded.

The sky darkens outside. Jackie must be wigging out. I hope she hasn't called Mom. I can't bear to think what state my mother is in if she believes I was abducted.

"We should get back," I say.

Aster doesn't react. *Aster*...Not sure what weirds me out more, the fact that he's named Aster too, or the fact that he's the twins' long-lost father.

"They'll be so excited to meet—"

"No."

"What?"

"No, Joshua. I can't."

"Can't what? Be their father? It's not a choice...it's a fact."

"I already have a family." His voice sounds as shrill as Ivy's when she freaks out over something.

"But they need you. Their mother, she isn't...well."

"Not my problem."

I feel like he sucker-punched me.

"Besides, I bet Rose slept with a lot of men back then. They could be someone else's girls."

I toss my hands in the air. "They *look* like you!"

"They look like their mom."

I frown. Out of all the reasons not to claim paternity, that is the dumbest. Rose is pale and freckled and has limp hair. "They look nothing like their mother. Run a genetic test. You'll see."

His nostrils pulse. "I'm not running any genetic tests."

"So what? You're just going to drop me off by my car and disappear? You have a website. I know your car's—well, your wife's car's—license number. I know your phone number."

"Are you threatening me? Because I don't do well with threats." The sleeve of his black nylon jacket lifts an inch and reveals a streak of blue-black ink on his wrist. I bet the man's covered in tattoos.

I shift in my seat, suddenly uncomfortable sharing air with a gun-toting, tattooed ex-soldier. I bet he was a SEAL. "All I'm saying is if *I* can find you, *they* can find you."

"They'd have to know where to look."

He raises the gun, points it at me. The tendons in his hands shift underneath his skin.

I keep my shoulders squared and force the panic off my face.

He dips his head down again. "I also know where *you* live Josh. I know how much you care about your mom. I know your dad's working on a project for the Discolis." He pauses. "It's real easy to make death appear accidental."

The blood drains from my face.

"Now, you're going to forget you ever saw me. You're going to wipe our conversation out of that lively mind of yours, and you're going to tell everyone you tossed this gun in Wildcat Creek."

"Or what—you'll kill me?" I square my shoulders. "I wonder what your wife would think if she knew you refused to even meet your daughters. She'd probably take your kids— you know those two, sweet little boys you deigned to recog- nize—she'll take them away. What woman wants a man without balls?" I'm pushing him hard. With a gun in my face, it's a dangerous move. But the twins have wanted to find their father for so—

Aster's arm locks around my neck, and the gun presses against my temple. The metal tip is cold, and pulses. Or maybe it's my forehead that throbs. Air trickles sluggishly through my throat, tacky like cough syrup, and soon I start gasping. I try to move, but he jams the gun harder. It'll probably leave a bruise. Unless he pulls the trigger. A bruise will be the least of my worries then.

"Going to shoot me to shut me up?" I wheeze.

"It would be a good solution, but I have a better one that doesn't require reupholstering yet another car."

When he mentioned his car was in the shop, I imagined he meant it was banged up, not soiled with blood and guts.

Chills fire up my spine and spread to my arms. I think of Mrs. Redd, of how brave and smart she was to keep her daughters a secret from a man like him. Not that one right erases the sum of her wrongs, but at least now—if I ever make it out of this car—I'll be able to share air with her without wishing her dead.

Aster speaks to me slowly, or maybe his words sound slurred because of how little oxygen is hitting my brain. "If *anyone* ever comes knocking on my door...be it the police or one of the Redd women...then I'll pay one of your parents a surprise visit."

I stare at the man holding me at gunpoint, and the knot of feelings untangles until only one sentiment is left: disappointment. "You don't deserve them."

Keeping the gun leveled on my face, he relaxes his grip on my neck and reaches over me for my door handle. He clicks it open, then shoves me out so hard, I stumble out and flop to my knees. I cough, retch, cough some more. The door swings shut, and then the car swerves out of the construction site.

I twist my neck, massage it. I spit. Hatred and anger thicken inside me, restoring some of my dignity.

Finally, I stand up.

I have no clue where I am, yet I know I can find my way back to the twins just like I knew I could uncover the origin of the gun.

As I walk, I kick Aster Colson out of my head.

Rid myself of his voice that sounded too much like Ivy's.

Purge my mind of his face that looked too much like Aster's.

I kick a pebble out of my way, and it arches and plummets noiselessly back down, vanishing in a sea of other upturned rocks. Like everything else in this life, what comes up must go down. I'll forget Aster Colson like I've already forgotten that stupid pebble.

EPILOGUE

DECEMBER 21, 2013

Josh and I have been dating for four glorious months.

I used to wish time would move faster, but not anymore. Now I wish each minute lasted a month.

I stand beside him in Maggie's candle-lit bakery, rubbing my clammy hands on the white-and-gray *ombré* dress he bought me for my birthday. He gave it to me merely an hour ago and instructed me to wear it right away. I told him it was too nice, too much for me. He shut me up with a kiss.

Stephanie, who's waiting for Ivy next to a little group of my sister's friends, glances my way. She smiles. She probably feels like she has to. After all, this party is for me, too.

"You think she's coming?" I ask Josh, tearing my eyes away from the hot-pink tulle eyesore Stephanie's sporting.

"Your sister? Miss a party? Especially a party in her honor?" He rolls his eyes. "Of course she's coming."

"I'm not talking about my sister."

He steals my hand from my side and clasps it between his soft, warm palms. "It's your birthday."

"She's missed a lot of them."

Ever since I discovered Mom's hidden treasure—a bunch of fabric rolls—she has avoided me. Not that I've set foot inside my home since the incident. I always idle out front in my car as I wait for Ivy.

I drive my sister to school every morning and drive her back every afternoon so she never has to take the bus or hike the now-frozen, blustery streets.

For months now, the only contact I've had with Mom is visual—through the veranda window. She sits in front of her sewing machine while I sit in front of my steering wheel. We watch each other until Ivy appears. I think Mom regrets alienating me. Or at least I hope she does. I don't dare ask Ivy because what if I'm wrong? What if Mom appreciates my absence?

Sometimes, ignorance truly is bliss.

"There they are," Josh murmurs.

I stiffen as Maggie parks in front of the bakery, then peer through the darkness to make out the number of bodies in the car.

I only see two.

Mom didn't come.

Josh wraps an arm around my waist and pulls me tighter against him, but I press him gently away because his parents are here. They know we're dating, but I'm still squeamish about PDA around them.

As my sister enters the glowing bakery, Stephanie, Sean, and her other friends squeal her name and capture her in giant hugs. They act as though they haven't seen her in days, as though they weren't just sitting next to her in class hours ago.

Finally, Ivy makes it to me. She takes in my dress and her mouth gapes a little. "Where did you get that?"

I try to answer her, but my emotions have tangled around my vocal cords.

Josh must have answered her question because Ivy says, "You have really good taste for a man."

"Not sure whether to take that as a compliment or not."

Ivy winks at him. "Definitely a compliment. I doubt my farmer husband will give me such pretty dresses. He'll probably give me overalls or cowboy boots."

"What farmer husband?" I ask.

Ivy and Josh exchange a conspiratorial look.

I feel left out, and it hurts. "Did you get married?"

"Of course not!" Ivy tells me about Mom's fortuneteller.

A prickling sensation bubbles behind my breastbone. Does Ivy know Mom never asked about me? "Why didn't she come?"

My question leeches the rosiness from my sister's skin. "She had to finish a project." My twin tucks a long, silky strand of hair behind her ear. "Christmastime is always busy for her."

Her lie vibrates in my bones. She's making excuses for Mom. I blink away tears. Why do I even care? I'm eighteen. As soon as tomorrow, I can emancipate myself from this woman.

Josh's father arrives with a platter full of rainbow-colored glasses. "Who wants to try one of my sparkling mocktails?"

Ivy pouts. "What? No champagne?"

"Not until you're twenty-one, young lady. Three more years to go," he says loudly. He tips his head toward Jackie who's helping Maggie light the candles on our cake.

When we turned fifteen, Stewart let us try beer. Sometimes, when Maggie's not paying attention, he'll sneak us a sip of his wine.

Ivy rolls her eyes, then goes for a pink glass, but he says, "Take the blue." And then he tells me, "Yours is the green, Aster."

I frown. Ivy wears a matching expression.

"Yellow for you, Josh."

Ivy picks the blue glass off the platter and takes a sip. Her frown transforms into a smile.

He whispers, "I added a splash of champagne to yours, but don't you dare tell your friends. *Or* Jackie. I don't feel like being arrested tonight."

"You're the best," Ivy quips.

"Happy birthday, sweethearts," he says, kissing Ivy's cheek, then mine.

I think he's been sampling his "mocktails," because his jaw is ruddy and his eyes shiny.

He waltzes away, distributing colorful glasses to the people who've come to celebrate our birthday. Well, Ivy's birthday. If it had only been mine, none of them would have come.

I dip my lips into my glass. The bubbles burst against my palate, then descend like pop rocks down my throat. I don't really taste the champagne because of all the fruit juice mixed into it, but halfway through my glass, I feel it.

I've become as light as a soap bubble, and Mom's absence doesn't irk me anymore.

The room breaks out in song as Maggie carries a blazing

sheet cake decorated with tiny purple marzipan flowers and green buttercream leafy vines. Our namesakes.

Ivy sidles next to me and links her arm through mine while Josh holds his phone out to take pictures.

Everyone's still singing.

"Did you make a wish, sis?" Ivy asks.

I look over at Josh, then back at Ivy.

I wish for us to be together forever.

I nod. "You?"

She nods, after which we blow out the candles.

Everyone claps.

While Jackie and Maggie start cutting up the cake in even squares, Ivy hands me a small, giftwrapped present.

I blink up at my sister, flushing. "I didn't get you anything."

"You don't need to get me anything, Asty."

"I do."

"Open it."

I tear the paper open to find a glossy paperback. I suck in a breath, trace the title with my fingertip.

Hopeless.

"The bookstore lady said it was a really good love story," Ivy says as I flip to the back matter and devour the synopsis.

"Thank you so much." My voice sounds strangled. "Tell me something you want. Please."

She bites her lip. "There is *one* thing."

I hope I can afford it. Ivy likes pretty things.

"Can you promise not to file charges against Mom?"

The book slides out of my fingers.

Neither Ivy nor I move to pick it up.

"Please, Asty. Don't have Mom taken away because you can now. School will be over in six months, and then you can leave…"

Ivy says more words, but they're flushed out by the loudness of the ones she's just spoken.

You can leave.

Not *we.*

You.

I've never felt lonelier in my life. "She didn't even come tonight. She doesn't care about me."

Ivy touches my shoulder. "She had to work."

"Don't lie for her! If she'd shown up, I might've..."

"Might've what?"

I was about to say *forgiven her*, but that's not true. I could never forgive my mother for her cruelty. "Might've reconsidered," I finally say.

Ivy's nostrils flare. "Asty, she said she'd kill herself if they tried to take her away."

More than her cruelty, what I can't forgive her for is turning me into someone cruel, someone who wishes death upon another human being, someone who can drug a person to uncover their secrets without feeling guilt.

That is not who I want to be.

"Maggie said you could stay with them until the fall," Ivy says, "and then you'll live on a campus somewhere. You're so smart, you'll get a full scholarship. I'm sure of it..."

I chose not to apply to colleges—something I haven't told either Ivy or Josh—because I want to start working. I want to make money so I can afford my own place. And then I'll go back to studying.

Josh is suddenly next to us. "Your entourage requests your presence," he tells Ivy, nodding in Stephanie's direction.

Ivy studies me a long time, awaiting my answer. I don't give her one because I don't want to lie to my sister.

Not on her birthday.

She turns her attention to Josh, and silent words travel between them. Or maybe they speak. My ears are buzzing.

When Ivy goes to her friends, I walk toward the door of the bakery and step out into the freezing night. I hug my arms around me to keep the cold air off my bare skin.

The door chimes a second later. A heavy coat falls over my shoulders.

"What happened?" Josh asks.

I pull his coat tighter around my shoulders, but still I shiver. "Mom won."

A crease appears between his eyebrows.

"Ivy asked me not file any charges against her."

He takes this in slowly, thoughtfully. "You don't need to press charges. You can emancipate yourself now."

"But what about Ivy? Mom could hurt her…"

"Ivy's a big girl."

"I don't want to do this alone," I croak.

"I'm right here." He pulls one of my hands away from my arm and twines his fingers through mine, then repeats the motion until both my hands are trapped in his.

Warmth flashes through me.

I love this boy so much.

If only his declaration could wipe away the pain of Ivy's wish.

Blinding headlights flood the street and then a car drives slowly by the bakery.

A dark green Jeep.

I inch toward Josh. I wish I was fearless, but I'm full of fears. "Mom's friend is back." My whisper curls like smoke through the frigid air.

Josh, who had his back to the road, spins around.

Mom made a friend in her shrink's waiting room, a friend whom she paid to buy a gun in my name. Jeep-lady swore to Josh she'd helped Mom because, being a single mother herself, she understood Mom's fears of living in a ground floor apartment unarmed.

"Why is she back?" I whisper again.

He shields me with his body until the car has vanished in the dark night. "Wasn't her." His voice is hard. He turns back toward me. "It wasn't her, Aster."

I run my gaze over his face a great many times to figure out if he's telling me this to reassure me or if it's the truth. "Maybe she doesn't believe you tossed the gun."

"I swear it wasn't her. I know the license plate by heart. It was another Jeep."

He pulls me into his arms and nestles his nose against my hair.

"No one's going to hurt you anymore. No one. That's my birthday present to you. To always protect you."

I lay my cheek in the crook of Josh's neck and smile. "You know, when I dream of my father, I dream he says those exact words to me." Josh's quick pulse nips my ear. "You think he would've protected me if he'd known about me?"

Josh doesn't say anything for so long I wonder if he's heard my question. I'm about to ask him again when he says, "You don't need a father. You have me."

Underneath the flapping pink awning and the canopy of stars, without caring who's watching us, I kiss him. "You know what I wished for before blowing out my candles?" I ask him once I've pulled away.

"Don't tell me or it won't happen."

Even though I burn to tell him, I swallow down my wish and lock it deep inside of me.

2 YEARS LATER

Our mother used to say that Ivy sucked all the good from the womb and I was left with the scraps. I hate to think she was right about anything, but my twin sister is exceptional.

"You're going to do so well," I tell Ivy, squeezing her hand.

"No touching," barks the guard watching over us.

It's just the two of us in the visitation room.

Ivy yanks her hand out of mine. "I don't know about *so well*, but I'm going to do my best." She links her fingers together in a business-like manner. "Has Josh come to see you yet?"

"No."

"He told me he spoke to your warden about letting you watch the show. You have his permission to look at it whenever you want."

I give her a weak smile. "That'll be the highlight of my day."

She runs her nail underneath the peeling, synthetic wood surface of the table.

"I'm happy you came to see me," I say.

Her gaze sticks to the tabletop. It's as though she doesn't dare look up at me. I think she's afraid to cry. "Was it really an accident, Aster?" Her voice is so faint that I have to strain to make out her words.

"Yes."

"You promise me—"

"Yes," I say. "Stop worrying about this. By the time you come home, it will be ancient history."

She bites her lip.

"Now go *make* history," I tell her.

"I'll probably be disqualified after the first round."

I shake my head. "Can you stop putting yourself down? You are *so* talented. So much more than all the other contestants."

"But this isn't only about talent."

If only I could curve the outer corners of her lips into a smile like I do at work with my computer cursor.

When her eyes twitch down to my hands, I slip both inside my jumpsuit pockets. "There's something I wanted to give you before the show," I tell her.

"What?"

"Just a little present."

"What is it?"

"If I tell you, it'll ruin the surprise." I drop my voice to a whisper. "It's in my underwear drawer. Where I kept my baby teeth."

She stays silent and still for so long that I shift around on the rigid iron chair. Suddenly, she stands. "I have to go home to pack."

"Already?"

She nods. "Before I go, though, you have to sign something for me." She heads over to the guard stationed in the corner.

As I watch her, the tips of my coarse curls brush against my gray jumpsuit. Ivy's hair is much longer than mine, and much softer. She styled mine once like hers—she even tried to teach me—but I have no patience with brushes and serums and creams. Besides, as much as I love my twin, at nineteen, we're past the age where it's cute to look identical.

After a quick exchange, she returns with his pen. She digs out a folded piece of paper from the back pocket of her skinny jeans and smooths it out on the desk. "The show sent me some extra forms to fill out. They need the signature from my next of kin in case something goes wrong."

My mouth goes dry. "It's an art competition...what could go wrong?"

"It's just a formality, Asty." She sticks the pen in my hand.

"But—"

"Nothing will go wrong." Her gaze softens. She knows I can never say no to her when she looks at me like that. "I promise."

I push out the breath I'm holding and study the paper. It's all fine print.

Ivy points to the signature line. "I've already read it. It's legalese. Disclaimers. The usual."

I bite my lip, and look back up at her. She's checking the

round white wall clock, so I hurry to scratch my name on the dotted line. "Here."

She tugs the sheet away from me and folds it back into her pocket. "Are you eating? You look skeletal."

I study the sharpness of my wrist bones. They do look like they're about to pierce my skin.

When she doesn't sit back down, I say, "It's time, isn't it?" I don't want her to leave, even though I encouraged her to go.

She nods.

I stand up, hoping for a hug, but instead, she lifts the pen from my hand and walks over to the guard to return it.

Over her shoulder, she calls out, "You take care, all right, Asty?" Her voice catches on my name.

I smile even though I didn't get my hug. Just like she didn't give me one yesterday when she came to visit. Maybe with the whole "no-touching-the-prisoner" rule, she doesn't know she's allowed to hug me on her way out. I keep the smile on my face long after she's gone, just in case she returns. She doesn't, but I don't hold it against her. Ivy has trouble with separation.

She was a mess when Mom was committed fifteen months ago. She was an even bigger mess when I was arrested.

KEEP READING NOW . . .

ACKNOWLEDGMENTS

The **Cold Little Games series** started with *Cold Little Games* (previously titled *The Masterpiecers*), which has now become the second book in the series. You must wonder how a first book became a second book? Well, the answer's simple: I wanted my readers to get to know Aster and Ivy before they became famous and to see where they came from. It took me signing up to be part of a wonderful mystery and thriller boxed set (MURDER & MAYHEM) to make this happen.

Now, onto the real reason for this part of the book. I'd like to thank, you, dear reader, for spending time with Aster and Josh. I hope you've enjoyed their tale and will look for the next episode in their lives.

I'd like to tell my beta-reading pit crew how thankful I am for the time they took out of their busy lives to read and critique my work. Your opinions and insights mean the world to me. So thank you, Theresea, Katie, Vanessa, Marina, and Astrid.

Sarah (my fabulous cover designer) and Jessica (my

extraordinary editor), thank you both for your attention to detail. No book is allowed out into the world without going past the two of you.

And finally, my crazy, loud family, I love all of you (more than I like writing, I promise!).

ALSO BY OLIVIA WILDENSTEIN

PARANORMAL ROMANCE

***The Lost Clan* series**

ROSE PETAL GRAVES

ROWAN WOOD LEGENDS

RISING SILVER MIST

RAGING RIVAL HEARTS

RECKLESS CRUEL HEIRS

***The Boulder Wolves* series**

A PACK OF BLOOD AND LIES

A PACK OF VOWS AND TEARS

A PACK OF LOVE AND HATE

A PACK OF STORMS AND STARS

***Angels of Elysium* series**

FEATHER

CELESTIAL

STARLIGHT

***The Quatrefoil Chronicles* series**

OF WICKED BLOOD

OF TAINTED HEART

ABOUT THE AUTHOR

USA TODAY bestselling author Olivia Wildenstein grew up in New York City, the daughter of a French father with a great sense of humor, and a Swedish mother whom she speaks to at least three times a day. She chose Brown University to complete her undergraduate studies and earned a bachelor's in comparative literature. After designing jewelry for a few years, Wildenstein traded in her tools for a laptop computer and a very comfortable chair. This line of work made more sense, considering her college degree.

When she's not writing, she's psychoanalyzing everyone she meets (Yes. Everyone), eavesdropping on conversations to gather material for her next book, baking up a storm (that she actually eats), going to the gym (because she eats), and attempting not to be late at her children's school (like she is 4 out of 5 mornings, on good weeks).

Wildenstein lives with her husband and three children in Geneva, Switzerland, where she's an active member of the writing community.

Places you can find me:
www.oliviawildenstein.com
press@oliviawildenstein.com